I0622356

"I threw myself off the plinth, twisting one ankle in the process, and heedless of the pain began running toward the gateway. Halfway back, I turned to discover a dozen or more of the creatures in pursuit, converging on me from various hiding places among the ruins. I quickened my pace as much as possible, spurred to even greater efforts by the sudden realization that the opening was shrinking visibly. I had only a few seconds to cover the intervening ground or I might have been trapped there!"

From "The Managansett Horror"

Managansett Press

Don D'Ammassa is the author of:

Horror
Blood Beast
Servant of Chaos*
Caverns of Chaos*
Wings over Manhattan
The Gargoyle
That Way Madness Lies*
Little Evils*
Passing Death*
Date with the Dark*
The Devil Is in the Details*
Living Things*

Science Fiction
Scarab*
Haven*
Narcissus*
Translation Station
The Sinking Island*
Alien & Otherwise*
Wormdance*
Sandcastles*
Carbon Copies*

Mysteries
Murder in Silverplate*
Dead of Winter*
Death at the Art Gallery*
Death on the Mountain*
Death on Black Island*

Fantasy
The Kaleidoscope*
Elaborate Lies*
The Maltese Gargoyle*
Perilous Pursuits*
Multiplicity*

Nonfiction
The Encyclopedia of Science Fiction
The Encyclopedia of Fantasy and
Horror
The Encyclopedia of Adventure Fiction
Masters of Detection Vol I*
Masters of Detection Vol II*
Architects of Tomorrow Vol I*

*published by Managansett Press

SHADOWS OVER R'LYEH

Don D'Ammassa

"Dark Paris" first appeared in *Extremes*, 2000
"Dark Providence" first appeared in *Return to Lovecraft Country*, 1997
"The Dunwich Gate" first appeared in *Terminal Frights*, 1995
"The Managansett Horror" first appeared in *Terminal Frights*, 1997
"Parting Shot" first appeared in *The Book of Dark Wisdom*, 2004
"Bad Soil" first appeared in *Singer of Strange Songs*, 1997
"Shadow Over R'leyh" first appeared in *Pulphouse*, 1991
All other stories appear for the first time in this volume.

Managansett Press First Edition 2015

SHADOWS OVER R'LYEH

CONTENTS

DARK PARIS

I was only supposed to be a civilian observer, but when the faint dark blur in the center of a fleecy cloud resolved itself into the shape of a zeppelin, the situation took on a much more personal aspect.

We were patrolling off the French coast, watching for infiltrators who used small boats to bypass the trench system and strike at the Allied supply lines. To this purpose the *Tenacity* was fitted with a forward battery of light guns, capable of sinking only the smallest of vessels, and a radio to call for help if we chanced upon something larger. Occasionally we sailed east and tried to glean useful intelligence about German troop movements, but either there weren't many or they were well concealed from the sea, because we never sighted anything larger than a small patrol. There was talk that the German High Fleet might try to break out again, though my companions were skeptical. I was of two minds on the subject. They'd run for shelter quickly enough after Jutland, but not before they'd dealt the British a painful blow. Unquestionably the British fleet was numerically superior, but not large enough to cover every possible attack route.

Me, I'm an American, Ted Connolly by name, officially retired from the military and employed by an entrepreneurial company involved in weapons development. Unofficially I represent an informal, clandestinely funded government agency trying to anticipate the future. President Wilson still preaches neutrality, but there are those within his administration who believe it's inevitable that the States will be drawn into the conflict. So I was asked to "temporarily" resign my commission and gather a little low level intelligence, evaluate the tactics of both our potential friends and their opponents. Others like myself actually enlisted in the RAF or served with the expeditionary forces on the Continent.

Strasser's zeps had been harassing the British for months, but their effect was more psychological than material. Other than one damaging raid on London, the airships had proven themselves surprisingly ineffective. Although the British had yet to cause any serious damage to the raiders, the officers I had spoken to were contemptuous of the German commanders.

"Half the time they drop their bombs in the ocean, and the rest end up in empty fields," insisted Captain Mayhew, whose acquaintance I cultivated when we were ashore because of his loquacious nature. "The crews sit around sucking oxygen out of tubes while the captains compose glorious stories of their exploits for the German press."

He was probably right, but the psychological impact was much more significant. Even in the smaller towns, unlikely targets for zeppelin raids, there was palpable terror at the thought of those great looming monstrosities hiding in the clouds, hovering unseen in the darkness and dropping ordinance on unsuspecting victims. Their virtual invulnerability heightened the sense of menace; heavier than air craft require long periods to climb to the necessary 20,000 feet elevations from which they could effectively attack the zeps, long enough for their quarry to hide among the clouds. I'd also observed a decidedly insular mentality among the British, who have relied so long on the enormous moat known as the English Channel that they panic at the thought their greatest defensive advantage has become irrelevant.

Captain Henderson had already rung up the engine room for more power and was turning away from the airship. The forward gun crew was elevating their weapons, but it was an empty gesture. We hadn't the range to loft a shell more than half the height required.

Able Seaman Howley emerged from belowdecks and stood at the rail beside me, squinting unnecessarily in the fading sunlight. "Do you suppose she sees us, mate?"

I glanced about at the unusually calm ocean. "She will if she looks down, Malcolm. There's not much cover for us to hide behind."

"Unnatural is wot it is, mate. Floating around in the bleedin' sky like that. Not an honorable way to fight at all is what I call it."

Henderson had us turned back toward the English coast by now, and our speed was increasing. The airship had apparently turned as well, setting a converging course that promised us a better view of the enemy. Despite the implied threat, I was frankly curious.

This was, after all, part of what I had been sent to do. It occurred to me that we were an unlikely target, an armed merchant ship of no great size and difficult to hit. On the other hand, there was some truth to my friend Mayhew's contention that many of the German captains were quite content to drop their bombs at the first opportunity, and I had no desire to risk being a casualty, however unlikely the event.

We were not built for speed and the airship was assisted by a favorable wind that augmented her multiple engines. As the minutes sped by, the gap continued to close, and just before dusk fell we were able to discern the forward gondola tucked snugly under the body of the vessel. Her markings indicated she was the LZ47, one of the newer ships with more powerful engines.

"She'll lose us in the darkness, likely," suggested Howley, more to reassure himself than to convince me. We were running full out with but a single light showing, but inexorably our pursuer gained upon us.

Captain Henderson walked around the deck, encouraging the men in his mildly pompous fashion. "Steady on, gentlemen. We'll outrun them handily as soon as the wind changes."

But luck wasn't with us. There'd been intermittent problems with the engines on our last patrol, fixed - or so we'd been told - by a quick overhaul while we were in port. We were straining our eyes to make out the shape of the Dover coast when a single sharp bang sounded from somewhere below, followed by a column of smoke that boiled furiously from belowdecks. I was standing near the bow when it happened, and as soon as I recovered my wits, I noticed that the trough of water we were creating had suddenly diminished in size.

"We're slowing!" I called unnecessarily. The rest of the crew were rushing about, and three men with faces blackened by smoke emerged onto the deck, coughing and gesturing wildly behind them.

We were fortunate in that there was little fire and that handled ably by the crew. One of the boilers had shattered along some undetected flaw line, however, and our speed continued to drop. The zeppelin had disappeared into another cloud bank but my last sight of it was less than reassuring. The distance had closed appreciably and barring a change in our circumstances, she could be directly above us in a matter of minutes.

Captain Henderson paced nervously back and forth while the chief engineer made his report. At best we could manage halfspeed, which meant we could not outrun the Germans. Adding to our difficulties was collateral damage. The rudder controls began responding sluggishly, evidence of further mechanical failure. Evasive tactics would be more difficult to manage. I followed Henderson's eyes when he looked up at the sky, where a formation of thick cloud concealed our antagonist, but as if in response to that gesture, the greater portion began to move away and we saw the nose of the zeppelin as it broke out into the open. It had narrowed the gap appreciably.

"Doesn't look so big, does it, mate?"

Howley's voice betrayed his uncertainty and I felt a momentary resentment, made no effort to conceal my exasperation. "It's three kilometers up, Malcolm."

And so the ponderous chase continued.

There could be no doubt now that the German was coming for us. Henderson turned to starboard, hoping that the airship would continue toward the coast and whatever target it had been ordered to attack. As luck would have it, there was a flash of lightning from inland, which apparently further discouraged the zeppelin's captain from his original course. Since we were the only other target in sight, he continued to follow.

For the next few minutes we made some headway, but then the wind must have shifted or the aircrew coaxed some additional power from the engines because the zeppelin seemed almost to leap across the sky in our direction. She had surrendered a good part of her altitude and lowered an observer's chair on a long cable from amidships, but this was now being wound in as the air had grown so turbulent that the occupant was in danger of being pitched out at any moment.

"Why don't they shoot?" Howley muttered querulously, his eyes shifting back and forth between the zeppelin and the gun crew. As if in answer, they did swivel the guns and fire a few rounds, but it was evident to everyone that we didn't have the range, and Henderson ordered them to desist.

"The muzzle flashes make us easier to see, gentlemen," he explained quietly.

They dropped their first bomb shortly thereafter, probably a five hundred pounder that hit the water fifty meters behind and to port. We turned sharply away, but even so the second bomb halved the distance and the third threw a wall of water crashing down onto the stern.

Some of the men rushed below, as if that provided any protection from the death falling upon us. For my own part, I wanted nothing to do with those cramped quarters. If this was to be my death, I would face it in the open. I looked up and saw the next bomb fall, and at first I was convinced that it would hit us directly amidships, but we'd slowed a bit more and they overflew us. The bomb struck ahead and to starboard, uncomfortably close but doing us no hurt. I noticed another object falling, stepped back just as it struck the deck almost within arm's reach.

That was the moment in which I learned what it was like to face your own death. Even the smallest of the German's bombs would have done for us then, because I was standing directly over the ship's magazine. Certainly I'd have had no chance of surviving. I waited for the flash and the roar and the pain and the cessation, but none of them came. Blinking, I wondered if we'd been hit by a dud, but then I looked down and saw the broken thing lying there and realized it was the illfated observer, plucked from his post and cast down upon us. Overhead, the cable and its terminal cage whipped back and forth in the increasingly turbulent wind.

The sky had opened up into a vast vault. The clouds which had obscured the zeppelin were gone now, but an even larger system covered the entire area like the interior of a domed cathedral. Lighting flashes in the distance reflected off the clouds and bathed the world in an eerie, softly blue light. Against that background, the zeppelin was much more visible than earlier, its oblong shape limned with St. Elmo's Fire. It was almost directly overhead and much larger, having apparently surrendered much of its altitude in order to improve the chances of hitting us. Another bomb dropped as I watched, showering us with a fresh wave. One piece of shrapnel struck our aerial and took out our communications, and another piece hit the rail inches from my hand. The impact jarred my grip loose, my feet went out from under me, and then I was in the water.

I don't remember the next few minutes very well. The impact partially stunned and disoriented me, and the shock of the cold

Channel water was not sufficient to immediately restore my senses. Fortunately, instinct took over and I managed to tread water until my vision became relatively clear and the worst of the fog cleared from my head.

I was alone. It had begun to thunder loud enough to drown out the sound of the *Tenacity*'s engines if they were still nearby. I heard one great roar that might have been another bomb or a particularly robust peal of thunder, but in any case the *Tenacity* was nowhere in sight.

I had little hope of swimming the remaining distance to Dover, but I was resolved to make the attempt, despite having no idea in which direction to strike out. I knew the stars well enough to take a rough heading, but the cloud cover was complete and impenetrable. Dismayed, I was afraid lest I choose the wrong direction and worsen my situation, even though I was near certain to die if I did nothing at all.

How long this funk lasted I have no way of guessing, but I suspect it was something less than half an hour before I saw a large shape looming in the sky. At first I thought it was just another lowering cloud, but then a certain regularity of feature caught my attention and I realized that it was the zeppelin, much descended, approaching me broadside where it was driven by the wind. Her engines still labored mightily, but the growing storm's power dwarfed anything built by mere mortals. Backlit by the still nearly luminescent sky, she seemed a toy, albeit a magnificent one, a child's balloon of unprecedented size. Her struggle to make way against the headwind was nearly successful, because she drifted back very slowly and as she did so, a flash of lightning revealed my only chance to escape the fate to which I'd begun to resign myself.

Perhaps thirty meters away, the observation cage was splashing through the heaving waves, still attached to the zeppelin's undercarriage by a metal cable. Its course would bring it past me at some distance, but not so far that I might not have a chance of intercepting it. Without debating further, I began to swim with all the strength and speed I could muster.

My arms and legs protested, for they were already wearied by the extended period I'd managed to remain afloat, but I ignored the pain and kept on. I would have time to rest afterward, one way or another. The pattern of stroke and breathe became the center of my universe, and I concentrated so intently that when it finally occurred to me to pause and get my bearings, I found I'd slightly overshot my mark and had to swim back briefly to place myself squarely in what was the most likely position. Fortunately the lightning was at its peak and I could check my bearings every few seconds. The airship drifted directly overhead but I was terrified that I would lose sight of the drifting cage at the critical moment and miss my last chance of escape. Fortune smiled on me however and I snagged it with surprising ease, felt myself lifted partially out of the water, then smashed back down as the zeppelin climbed and fell in the grip of the air currents. We rose again and I swung myself inside, having no difficulty because one of the four sides was completely gone, leaving behind only three twisted metal joints where it had been torn away, presumably taking its erstwhile occupant with it.

I wrapped my arms through the grating of two separate sections, figuring that if another side suffered the same fate that I'd still have a chance of holding on. The wind became gustier and more chill and I began to shiver from exposure as well as exhaustion and shock. Fortunately, the zeppelin gained some altitude a short time later and lifted the cage and its newfound crew a healthy distance above the waves.

The rain was so heavy that the difference between dangling in the sky and floating amid the waves was negligible. The aerial pyrotechnics were ferocious enough to keep my adrenaline pumping, and that counteracted to some extent the chill that was seeping through my muscles. I believe I lost consciousness for some period of time, because when next the storm's fury abated somewhat, a flash of lightning revealed that we were passing over a heavily forested region.

I knew this had to be near the French coast, but there was no way of determining whether it was land held by friendly or enemy hands. Certainly the zeppelin crew would be attempting to fly eastward. Even if they couldn't reach one of the aerodromes, they might land in an open space, bleed off the hydrogen to deflate the gasbags, and avoid having their airship destroyed by the raging winds. The weather might well have foiled their efforts, however, because the prevailing wind had been toward the southwest earlier in the evening and they would perforce have been driven before it.

My body was numb with cold and my thoughts were sluggish, but I still remember the next few seconds so clearly that my hands are shaking even as I write this. The storm was so intense that the play of lightning was incessant. Sheer luck had spared the airship up till now, but suddenly a bolt struck the gondola and a fountain of blue light splashed out in every direction. The charge traveled down the tether to where I crouched and in the moment before I lost consciousness I was convinced that this was my death.

It wasn't. I recovered my wits some time later. My arms and legs were stiff with cramps, but they were still wrapped through the walls of the observation cage. Miraculously, we were still aloft. The storm had largely subsided although an occasional lightning strike revealed that we were still passing over land. I wondered how much time had passed; the night air smelled of ozone and some underlying, more unpleasant scent. There wasn't the faintest hint of the ocean.

Another flash revealed that we were even lower than I thought. The cage in which I sheltered drifted only a few meters above the highest of the trees, and I could dimly see the shapes of buildings here and there, although they seemed distorted. At the time, I dismissed this as a trick of the eyes, but later I was to discover otherwise. Our progress continued for another half hour or so, during which the rain gradually stopped, although the air remained turbulent. The wind buffeted me from different angles, and the zeppelin above apparently fared no better because we abruptly descended low enough that branches began to brush against the bottom of my cage, one catching in the fabric of my pants and tracing a long though mercifully superficial scratch across one calf. I forced myself to move, climbed entirely inside the cage, hoping that its walls would provide some protection.

Then we were past the trees and traveling above a fully lighted city.

I had visited Paris several times prior to the war, and once accompanied Paul Garimond on a balloon flight on a particularly clear night. I recognized the same arrangement of rivers below me now, the same pattern of development. But this wasn't the Paris I knew. Instead of the sparkling river of light one would expect, there was a subdued yellowish blue glow like a giant bruise that seemed to have no distinct source. For the first few moments I thought the harsh treatment I'd recently experienced might be causing hallucinations, because the buildings below me only remotely resembled human artifacts. They were coarser in detail, asymmetrical blocks that set my nerves on edge, and the few figures I spied moving among them seemed furtive, and they were not entirely human either. I was only half convinced that my eyes were telling me the truth until the airship started a sharp descent, half turning in the process, and I saw the Eiffel Tower.

Or what stood in its place in this dark world.

It was roughly the same size and shape, but unlike the magnificent tower with which I was familiar, this obscenity was a blatantly phallic edifice that towered over the city. It was a closed structure whose skin seemed to be in constant movement, an incessant writhing that I soon realized was caused by the myriad creatures that swarmed over its structure, their misshapen bodies a parody of flesh. Then we dropped behind a row of the cyclopean buildings, the cage smashed into one of the structures, and I was thrown from my perch, landing with jarring force on the roof below me. The airship continued onward and downward, and I lost sight of it.

I lay stunned for a short period during which the lighting changed appreciably, the blue giving way to a rusty red that teased at rather than dispersed the shadows. A bloody sun rose behind a sheath of viscous clouds on the horizon. As sensation slowly returned to my limbs, I puzzled over my situation. How could the night have passed so swiftly? Admittedly I had lost consciousness at least twice, but it was inconceivable that the zeppelin had drifted all the way to Paris so quickly. I was later to learn that my new environment was a flawed copy whose geography was relationally the same although compressed into a much smaller space. Likewise time either flowed differently or this Earth pursued a different orbit, because the days were shortened by approximately one third from those I knew.

Blood circulated painfully through my cramped limbs and the bizarre "daylight" brought no warmth, but eventually I felt well enough to explore my surroundings. I crouched at the edge of the roof and peered down into a dingy alley that ran beneath my perch. It was too far to jump, but a few meters away the structure bowed like a swaybacked horse. I slid down the decline and from its lowest point was able to drop to ground level.

I'd been aware of a faint hum like that of distant traffic for some time, but now an eerie keening arose from somewhere in the distance, almost like an air-raid siren except that it sounded biological, not mechanical, an animal in distress perhaps. It continued for a moment or two, then trailed off. Except for a sudden nagging thirst, I actually began to feel better as I tentatively explored my surroundings. I covered the equivalent of three city blocks without seeing another living being, although on one occasion I glimpsed furtive movement at the end of a passageway, possibly a small animal.

I had a fairly good idea where I was despite the altered landscape. The Eiffel Tower, or its equivalent, had been off to the right just before the crash, but we hadn't passed over the Seine. I was pretty sure I was walking east, so that meant I should be coming up on the Tuileries soon. I had spent a glorious afternoon touring the gardens of the ruined palace, once home to Napoleon, and had lived in L'Hotel Des Tuileries for several weeks. Bewildered, and possibly still suffering from mild shock, I seized upon it as a starting point to determine what had happened to me, or the world, or both.

I was actually within the boundary of the Tuileries before I realized it, and only recognized my surroundings when the unmistakable silhouette of the Louvre emerged from the thick morning fog. The light had increased almost imperceptibly and it felt more like sunset than sunrise. I hesitated, gathered my wits, and realized I had emerged into a comparatively open area populated by a mix of statues and plantlife. But any resemblance to the magnificent gardens of my memory was purely coincidental. Most of what passed for shrubbery consisted of thick stemmed plants with tubular leaves intermixed with what seemed to be tufts of black, oily hair. There were thorns everywhere, wickedly sharp and measuring up to four inches long. Scattered among these were occasional larger growths, tree-sized, but inverted. A half dozen distinct trunks merged at eye level or above into a single mass from which spiky, distorted limbs spread horizontally into a chaotic canopy. There were flowers here and there as well, if those blood red structures resembling coiled intestines could be called such. The statues varied from almost comical mixtures of human and animal body parts to several that were overtly phallic, and when I placed my hand on one, it was warm and slightly resilient, as though carved from living flesh.

As I penetrated further into the garden, some of the flowers altered their position when I passed, as though aware of my presence. Unnerved completely by this observation, I turned to my right and headed toward the Seine. The tepid, stagnant air had made breathing difficult from the first, but now a deeper stench assailed me, growing stronger as I moved toward the river bank. I was tempted to turn back, but some perverse fascination led me onward.

The Seine was a roiling cesspool. It smelled of decay, but also of something stronger, a deeper, more basic kind of corruption. The river flowed sluggishly, perhaps inhibited by the thickness of its substance, which I cannot call water. Rather it had the consistency of partially coagulated blood. Small waves appeared occasionally, and sometimes they remained upright and stationary for several seconds before slowly subsiding. Pockets of gas erupted from the surface with small, unpleasant pops and hisses.

I was standing motionless above this obscenity when I sensed motion to my left. What appeared to be a human figure stood beneath a bloated tree perhaps fifty meters away. I raised a hand to wave, but as I did so, the figure turned and moved away down the Quai du Louvre, almost immediately disappearing into the fog. I hesitated only a few seconds before following. The figure had seemed evasive but not menacing, and no better course of action suggested itself.

I walked briskly forward for several minutes without sighting my quarry. On two occasions I stopped to listen, but the fog and the slimy carpet of moss that covered the ground muffled even my own footsteps. It never occurred to me to call out; there was something about this altered Paris that inhibited such a forthright action. Then I found myself in front of the Louvre, which externally at least seemed very much like the one I knew. Its doors yawned open and impulsively I altered course and stepped inside.

Even today, I find it difficult to recall what I saw within those walls. The galleries were laid out much as I remembered them, and many of the canvases bore familiar names - Degas, Manet, Monet - and their styles were the same. But the subject matter! Scenes of perverse sexual debauchery, torture, mutilation, and corruption. Rotting corpses performing a ballet. Picnickers barbecuing babies over an open fire. Males with impossibly large members impaling struggling women, or other men. People sitting in a tavern dining on their own entrails. And these are among the less unpleasant scenes, the ones I can bear to articulate. I moved from gallery to gallery in stunned horror and finally froze in front of a particularly grotesque frieze, my mind overwhelmed by the evil with which I was surrounded.

That's when Nelson tapped me on the shoulder.

I rounded on him with raised fists but he simply stood motionless until my alarm subsided to wariness. He seemed perfectly normal, a grizzled man of approximately my size and age, wearing tattered clothing and a calmness I interpreted as self confidence, though later recognized as resignation. His left hand hung loose at his side but his right was concealed inside the rags of his shirt.

"Easy, friend. You've nothing to fear from me." His accent was American, but an unusual one I couldn't place.

I lowered my arms, but remained wary. "Who are you? What is this place?'

"Nelson's the name, and why, this is France, of course." His laugh was totally devoid of humor. "All right, friend, I'll tell you the truth of it. This is Hell itself. You've crossed into the land of the dead, even though you're still alive. I've never had much use for preaching myself, but this place surely resembles the Damnation my daddy warned me about, devils and lost souls and all."

The things Nelson told me during the next few minutes were difficult to believe, but I was subsequently to discover that his account was accurate in virtually every detail. The world around me was a distorted version of the Earth with which I was familiar. It had been created by one or more of a race of inhuman creatures, about whom Nelson would say little. "The Old Ones are the masters of this world, Connolly, and not to be spoken of lightly. In fact, you'd be best advised to avoid attracting their attention in any way." These mysterious beings had once ruled the Earth, according to Nelson, and had been driven from our universe by another race. Now they dwelt in their own realm, waiting for the day of their return. "They dream this world, I believe, even though it's real to us. They can change things with a thought." And to prove his point, he removed his concealed hand and showed it to me.

There was a small, well formed mouth in the center of his palm, and his fingers, all eight of them, coiled and uncoiled bonelessly.

I recoiled and Nelson laughed again. "You'll see worse than this. And at least my body is still my own. I came through with two friends. One was taken by a Passenger. His body still walks around and even speaks occasionally, but there's a mass of coiled black wire inside him that works him like a carnival dummy. The other, well, he tried to get back home and they caught him and now he's up at the Tower being the bones for one of the Children." He wouldn't explain what that meant, but he did say that they'd been in an observation balloon during a sudden thunderstorm when they'd crossed over. They were visiting Paris at the time as part of a mission to convince the French to intervene on the side of the Confederacy.

"Nonsense," I protested. "That would make you at least seventy years old. Are you trying to tell me people don't age here?"

Nelson shrugged. "Some do, some don't. But time doesn't pass the same way as back home. I figure I've been here less than ten years, but it's hard to keep track. There's no seasons to speak of, no calendars, and the few kids - well, they aren't around long enough to grow up much."

Nelson brought me to his home, a single room in a nondescript misshapen building near in what should have been Montparnasse. There was a single slit window which he'd plugged with debris. "Best not to show a light," he explained. Some of the nearby buildings were similarly occupied, although most of the residents kept to the shadows and avoided us as well as each other. Nelson introduced me to two of the least furtive, a Frenchman named Fournier whose neck grew out of the center of his chest, and Gerda, a German woman who seemed entirely normal until she paused in mid sentence to vomit up what appeared to be human excrement.

"She ran into one of the Old Ones," Nelson explained later. "Her insides are all scrambled up. She has to sit on her food in order to eat." He left the rest to my imagination.

Nelson had fed me by now, and the nature of that food is best left undescribed. Suffice it to say that the residents of this altered Paris lived on a variety of noxious nutrients. Most of what I consumed during my stay was harvested from gardens like those of the Tuileries, but I also dined on occasional delicacies of dubious origin, including some harvested from the living.

"Old Giardeau keeps growing extra limbs. If we don't cut some of them off, he gets top heavy and can't walk right."

There were animals in this Paris, just as distorted as its human population, but they were few and fleet of foot and even when trapped, not always edible. "Killed a horse once. Damn thing broke its leg trying to get away. But when I tried to gut it, it was like a nest of snakes inside and they all slithered off before I had the presence of mind to try to catch any of them."

Nelson helped me to find a room of my own - a den really - and taught me how to forage for the less nauseating foodstuffs. We accumulated water in clay basins by shaking the morning dew from the spatulate leaves of a common bush. It had a sour undertaste and an oily texture, but I learned to ignore the taint and satisfy my thirst. After a few days, it almost seemed normal.

Tactfully, I avoided talking about Nelson's deformity until he brought it up himself, about two weeks after my arrival. He was complaining about the awkwardness of performing certain tasks with his malformed limb. "How did it happen?" I blurted out without thinking. "I mean, all of you," I gestured broadly, "you've all changed to some extent."

"Happens to everyone eventually. If you get spotted by an Old One, like Gerda did, it happens real fast and real drastic. Most of us, though, we just started changing a little bit at a time. Maybe it's something in the air, in the water, in the food. Doesn't matter. Eventually we all become a part of this place. You will too."

That's when I started pressing him about escape.

I'd tried before, but it was the only subject Nelson didn't like talking about. I asked about his friend, the one who'd been caught trying, and he put me off a couple of times, but eventually I wore him down.

"It's the Tower," he said grudgingly. "Did you ever notice it at night?"

I had. From Montparnasse, we could see the top half of the Tower fairly clearly, even in the darkness. Although there was no artificial light, it was sharply defined by a persistence electrical discharge that danced around its structure. From a distance, it seemed like St. Elmo's Fire.

"What about the Tower?"

"None of us really belong here, you understand. It's our nature to return to our own universe. But the Old Ones, they've sort of squeezed the interface down into one single spot, at least here in Paris. There's probably other ones elsewhere. Anyway, there's all this energy surrounding the gateway and it bleeds through both ways. Every one of us came through during an electrical storm, you know."

"So if there's a way back…"

"Why don't we use it?" For the first time since we'd met, Nelson was clearly angry. "Is that what you're thinking? That we're all cowards?" I waited for a few seconds and his anger dissipated like mist. "Some try it, but I don't think any of them ever succeeded. There are Guardians all around, covering the Tower from top to bottom. Passengers and Children and even worse things. You try, you get caught; you get caught, you get changed." He was silent for a few seconds, staring off into an unseeable distance. "And once you're changed, you're not really sure you want to go back." He raised his malformed hand and the lips parted to reveal tiny, perfect teeth. "What do you suppose they'd make of me back in the real world, or Gerda, or Hans, or any of the others?"

Despite Nelson's warnings, I set out the next day for the first of many scouting missions. I watched the Tower from both sides of the Seine, from the Avenue de la Bourdonnais and from the Champs Elysees. Undiscovered, I approached ever closer, though never sacrificing caution, and eventually found several vantage points from which I could reconnoiter effectively. The scenes I witnessed enacted in living flesh many of those I'd seen on canvas in the Louvre. The Passengers appeared human except on those rare occasions when wirelike black strands erupted from their bodies to sting their victims. The Children were giant mounds of translucent flesh sculpted over distorted human frames that still lived, completely immersed in the gelatinous substance of their captors. Other creatures resembled oversized manta rays, and it was these which were the most numerous, swarming over the superstructure of the Tower except in those places where electrical discharges flared.

I saw terrible things from my hiding places, including three attempts to reach the gateway. One young man with a prehensile tail bolted from cover toward the Tower and made it half way across the open ground before one of the Children swung an amorphous arm and beheaded him. The decapitated body became disoriented but continued to run back and forth, aimlessly, eventually disappearing behind a row of buildings. Another man was whipped to bloody shreds by two Passengers and a girl no older than twelve made it all the way to the Tower steps before being engulfed by one of the manta things, emerging a few seconds later with the flesh boiling away from her bones.

Much of the time, the guardians preyed on each other. The Children were prone to battling among themselves by scooping away gobbets of an opponent's flesh until the encapsulated human was accessible. Once the interior life was extinguished, the Child floundered about for some time, then slowly dissolved into a pool of slime. Similarly the Passengers frequently maimed the hosts of their fellows, although rarely to the point of incapacity. I once saw a Passenger desert its host, emerging as a pile of coiled black wires that slithered off into the underbrush in quest of a new host. From time to time, one of the mantas would disappear, eventually returning with a (more or less) human victim. I watched them pull out a man's limbs, one at a time, all eight of them. Other deaths were even less pleasant.

But I also saw my chance.

The Passengers and Children were few in number and there was no pattern or method to their activity. Sometimes they were spread fairly evenly around the tower, sometimes they tended to congregate on only two or three sides. The mantas were more problematic. They were far more numerous and they virtually engulfed the Tower. On the other hand, they seemed even more prone than the other two types to fight among themselves, and in their case it wasn't individual combat. Significant numbers of them engaged in spasmodic battles. There may have been two or more groups involved, but they all seemed identical to me. What I did see was a gap in the Tower's last line of defense while they were fighting.

All I had to do was wait for a favorable mix of events. If the mantas started one of their battles while the Passengers and the Children were leaving a reasonably open approach, there was a chance I could run to the Tower before they noticed me. I had no idea what to do once inside, but it was quite clearly my only hope. Each morning I checked my increasingly filthy body for signs of change, and each morning I breathed a sigh of relief to discover that I remained entirely human. I had no mirror, and the light was always dim and vaguely wrong, but I could count my limbs and digits, my internal processes appeared to be normal, and I hadn't sprouted tentacles or a tail or horns or a third eye. But it was only a matter of time, and I had secretly decided for myself that if the change started before I was able to return to my own world, then I would end my life here in this twisted version of Paris by throwing myself headfirst from the roof of the Louvre. If I could muster the nerve.

For three weeks my despair increased. On more than one occasion, two of the three conditions of escape were met. Either the Passengers and mantas were clear, or the Children and the Passengers, or the mantas and the Children, but never all three. I was considering an even more desperate attempt. The Children were the most powerful but slowest of my enemies; there was a chance, however slim, that I could weave my way through them if the Passengers and mantas were out of the way. But even as I prepared for what I believed was probably my death, the event for which I'd been waiting arrived.

I froze in disbelief for the first few seconds. Other than a single moribund Child and a wounded manta that lay floundering on the ground, there was nothing moving between me and the Tower's base. I scrambled to my feet, mentally wished Nelson the best of luck, and bolted out into the open. Somehow the Child sensed me even though it was facing in the opposite direction and it turned, but far too slowly. I was past it, my body operating on instinct as much as purpose. The wounded manta flopped in my direction, but apparently by chance rather than purpose. I swerved to my right and passed with room to spare. The shadow of the Tower fell across me and then I was running up a short flight of crumbling steps and under an enormous archway of twisted black metal.

Something tenuous resisted my advance, as though I'd run into heavy curtains, but I kept pumping my legs and it gave way and I was inside. A sudden bright spot of light popped up in front of me just as something dark and fast and menacing began descending from above, so I put my head down and kept running. The light grew and I smelled ozone and there was a sudden tingling sensation all over my body. Then the light changed and I was falling and before I had a chance to look around I hit the water.

And it was real water. Clear and clean and not even salt.

There's not much more to tell. A goatherder found me lying on the shore of Lake Turkana, half drowned, half crazy. He spoke reasonably good English, but it was a while before I could respond, and then I was so incoherent that no one paid much attention, even during the trip out of the Rift Valley and down to Nairobi, where I was given a private room at a surprisingly modern hospital. Surprising to me, of course, because I learned it was 1999, which made me well over a century old.

I'd say I look surprisingly good for my age, but that wouldn't be true. I don't look good at all. They won't let me have a mirror any more, and they keep me wrapped in useless gauze and bandages, more for the sake of the staff than for medical reasons, I'm certain. The change that I'd feared had already started when I made my desperate rush for freedom. A portion of the skin of my back had become transparent, revealing the flesh and organs beneath. By the time I reached Nairobi, the transformation had spread across most of my torso, and shortly after that the process was complete. Apparently some of the organs have changed as well, and they occasionally reposition themselves inside my body. I am now a monster so horrible that even the doctors avert their eyes, and the authorities politely but firmly refuse to release me, even though I am otherwise physically sound. I begin to understand now why Nelson and the others showed no interest in escaping from that bizarre other world. My deformities would not have made me a pariah there.

My room has a window, barred since my last suicide attempt. Through it I watch the skies, clear now, and my spirits only improve when dark clouds gather on the horizon and thunder makes the sky tremble. I know the odds are against it, but I have a bond with that other world and perhaps, just possibly, I might one day return to where I belong. There are some things even worse than Hell.

DARK PROVIDENCE

It all started when they moved the river. Moved it again, actually, back to its original course. The Providence River had been diverted to allow the development of the land at the foot of College Hill, but by the early 1990's, there was already growing interest in ripping up the Canal Street area and restoring the original watercourse.

No one could have realized the consequences, of course. The only man who might have warned them was long dead, buried in Swan Point Cemetery. His name was Howard Phillips Lovecraft.

Personally, I'm indifferent to the man's work, but Kerri was an addict. It was her only vice other than cigarettes, and she was trying to give those up. Kerri had read every word that Lovecraft had written, could quote long passages from memory. She collected alternate and foreign editions, many of which she would never be able to read. She'd spent thousands of dollars to acquire the original Arkham House collections and a complete run of Weird Tales. The walls of her bedroom were lined with Lovecraftiana, which had spilled over into the living room, den, even the bathroom. There were two long shelves of critical works, and two more with Mythos stories by other authors. She'd even spent several weekends in the John Hay Library, painstakingly copying the notes HPL had written in the margins of his own collection of magazines.

"Feel like doing something this weekend?"

We were standing in the parking lot at Eblis Manufacturing, the end of a long and frustrating week of inventory. Kerri looked blank for a moment, then smiled, a transformation that made me want to kiss her right on the spot.

"Sure, Danny. How about a picnic?"

"Sounds great. Roger Williams Park or Lincoln Woods?"

Her eyes shifted to one side and she bit her lip. "I was thinking about Swan Point."

I should have figured. I liked Kerri a lot, maybe a bit too much considering her abstraction from the real world. God knows I'd tried to lure her away from her obsession, but nothing seemed to work. At the art show, she remarked on similarities to scenes from Lovecraft stories, she interpreted concert music as possible soundtracks, and when I took her to a Pawsox baseball game, she carried a paperback collection in her purse and ignored what was happening on the field.

I knew better than to argue. "Sure, down on the river bank. Sounds great."

Actually, once we got past the obligatory visit to Lovecraft's grave, it really was pretty great. Kerri wore cut off jeans and a white halter top that drew my eyes like a magnet. The Brown University rowing team was practicing just offshore, but otherwise there was no one in sight. We found a shady spot under an oak tree and spread out the blanket, emptied our basket of tunafish sandwiches, apple juice, and miscellaneous finger food. After we'd eaten, Kerri lay back against the swell of a hill and stared out across the water, and I wanted her so badly I had to turn away.

"Feel like an adventure?"

"I feel like a turkey stuffed for Thanksgiving." I rolled over onto an elbow. "What did you have in mind?"

"They've been digging at the foot of College Hill, near the bus tunnel."

"Pedestrians aren't allowed down there."

She slapped the side of her thigh irritably. "That's part of what makes it an adventure. Besides, college kids go in all the time to party."

"Late at night, maybe. After the buses stop running."

"Yeah, that's when I thought we should go, around midnight."

I'd have gone just about anywhere alone in the dark with Kerri, but the bus tunnel through College Hill struck me as considerably less than romantic. I hesitated, not crazy about the idea, but not wanting to miss whatever chance might offer itself. "I thought it was all fenced off, to keep people away from the construction."

"Not all of it. They broke into an older section this afternoon and only had time to put up a barricade."

So I agreed.

"This isn't such a great idea." I moved the flashlight around, illuminating the yawning chasm in front of us. "There could be rats in here."

"Rats in the walls," she whispered. "They just cut away this part of the bank today. I was sitting up there watching," she gestured vaguely behind us. "When they broke through, there was a big cave-in. It was high tide and the water came rushing through, so they just plowed a berm up to contain it and shut down the site."

I felt a mild tremor of anxiety. "Doesn't sound particularly safe."

"Tide's out now." That was supposed to satisfy me, I guess. It didn't. I glanced around, searching for a way to back out of this expedition. When I looked back, Kerri was gone.

"Wait up!" The thin thread of her flashlight was already receding.

The footing was uncertain, a steep slope of crumbling shale and loose soil, plenty of clearance to either side but the ceiling was low enough that I had to duck from time to time. The gloomy darkness seemed to be fraying the edges of our flashlight beams. The air was heavy with moisture, chilly, clammy, and it smelled and tasted of mold, dust, corruption.

Kerri stopped suddenly, only a few meters ahead of me, and I breathed a sigh of relief, assuming she'd come to the far end of the cavity.

"Danny, come look at this!" There was a husky undertone in her voice, excitement, almost sexual. I tried to hurry, but the footing was so uncertain, it made little difference to my progress. I was so intent on avoiding a misstep that I bumped into Kerri without realizing how close I'd come.

"Easy. What do you make of this?"

"This" was a metal door anchored between two columns of rock. There was no clearance on either side.

"An old maintenance access, I'd guess. Or something left over from the original construction."

"Let's try to get it open."

"I don't think..." But it was too late. Kerri put the flashlight down, wrapped both hands around the handle, spread her feet and tugged. Loose earth shifted and fell but the door didn't move.

"Probably rusted in place. Let's get out of here; there's nothing more to see."

"Don't give up so easy. I think it moved a little bit. Maybe the two of us can shift it." There was a smear of dirt across the front of her halter top, exactly where I wanted to put my hands.

"All right."

Just before I decided to abandon the effort, the door shifted. Not much, only about an inch, but that was enough to dislodge a small avalanche of damp earth that rained down on us. I started to swear as I brushed away the worst of it.

"Don't be so anal. Let's get this open."

It was the first time I'd actually come close to losing my temper with Kerri, but I bit my tongue and joined her. A few minutes later, at the cost of more fallen dirt and a great deal of sweat, we had shifted it enough to let us pass through.

I didn't think that was such a great idea, but Kerri was not to be denied. "This is the first chance at a real adventure I've ever had and I'm not going to miss it. Who knows what we might find? There could be treasure...or dead bodies." She seemed to find both alternatives appealing.

"Or rats and spiders and centipedes," I countered.

"Are you coming or not?" She stepped forward into my flashlight beam. Her long blonde hair was matted with dirt, and there were broad streaks across her face. I'd have followed her into the mouth of hell.

Maybe that's what I did.

The chamber beyond the door wasn't very large. The two of us made a crowd inside. Kerri was so close, I fancied I could feel the heat of her body even through the mugginess. We played our flashlights around the chamber, but it seemed bare stone and earth, without content or meaning. Kerri shrugged and had half turned to go when I, to my eternal regret, looked more closely at the opposite wall.

"Wait a minute. There's something here." The texture of the soil was different and I reached out to touch it, jumped back in astonishment when my hand disappeared into what seemed to be solid earth.

"I don't see anything." Disappointed, Kerri had lost interest; her voice was impatient, irritable.

"Put your hand on the wall here. Tell me what you feel."

She hesitated, then took three quick steps across the chamber and stretched out her arm. It disappeared up to her wrist. "Cool!

How deep do you think it goes?"

"I don't know. It's some kind of optical illusion, I guess." I reached out again, this time lost sight of my arm up to the elbow. There was a faint tingling that might have been imagination. "Can't feel anything."

"Let me." And before I could say or do anything, Kerri stepped through the barrier. I was suddenly alone in the chamber.

"Kerri!" No answer. I was summoning the courage to follow when she reappeared.

"Oh, there you are! Where the hell did you go?"

"Where did I go? You're the one who vanished."

"Well, you weren't here a minute ago. Or at least..." She glanced back over her shoulder. "Hold my hand a minute."

I didn't need much prompting. Her fingers were cool but they were surprisingly strong. Strong enough to pull me off balance and through the barrier.

At least, that's what I thought happened. But the flashlight revealed that we were back where we'd started. "I don't get it."

"Wait." Kerri crouched, still holding my hand, and placed her flashlight on the floor. "Okay, here we go again." And for the second time she dragged me into the illusory wall.

And once again we were back where we'd started. Except that there was no flashlight on the ground.

"What's going on?"

"I thought I'd gotten turned around in the dark, but there really are two sides. They just look an awful lot alike."

But I distinctly remembered seeing a passage leading up toward the surface, and said so.

"So let's find out where it goes." She released my hand and vanished again before I could argue the point. What choice did I have? I followed her.

She'd already recovered the flashlight and was on her way up. It was a lot more difficult than coming down; the mud was slippery and there was nothing solid to hold onto for leverage. Both of us fell a couple of times and by the time we reached the top, we looked pretty awful.

Canal Street was a line of ravaged payment. I knew they'd been planning to demolish the roadway but hadn't realized how far they'd progressed. The city was quiet. It was well after midnight and

I couldn't even hear traffic sounds from the interstate.

We sat on a mound of asphalt and caught our breaths. Kerri admitted being disappointed, but her normal good humor prevailed and we were making fun of each other before long. Even in the darkness, we were pretty sorry looking, dripping filth, soaked with perspiration.

"I don't know how I let you talk me into this, Kerri. If anyone sees us like this, we'll never live it down."

She laughed at me. "You could have said 'no'. I didn't exactly hold a gun to your head."

"Yeah, well I've always wanted to do something dirty with you." It came out unbidden, and an uneasy silence interrupted our playful mood. The seconds stretched before Kerri broke the tension.

"My apartment's not far. You could take a shower."

I glanced down at my shirt. "I really need some clean clothes."

"There's a washing machine."

I chose my words carefully, hopefully. "That might take a while."

"I think we could find a way to pass the time."

I was so preoccupied with the possibility of finally realizing my favorite fantasy that it took a while to realize that something was wrong with the city. It was too dark for one thing. Hospital Trust Plaza and Fleet National were both completely dark. The streetlights were out. In fact, none of the skyscrapers showed lights; the only illumination seemed to originate closer to street level, out of our line of sight. It flickered, like fire. And it was quiet. A faint rumbling in the distance was probably highway traffic, though it sounded different, wrong.

We made our way across the construction site, which seemed far more extensive than I remembered. Surely they hadn't reached South Main Street already. And the Providence & Washington Insurance building was partially demolished; rubble covered the sidewalk and adjacent street.

"Something's wrong here."

"Yeah." Kerri's voice was tense. "What happened while we were down there? Power failure?"

At the next corner, we surprised someone. He appeared to be

a street person, almost as dirty as we were, clothes tattered, hair long and unkempt. Cadaverously thin, his clawed hands sorted through a pile of trash. It looked as though he meant to challenge us at first, but then he broke and ran off before we had time to react.

Vaguely disturbed, we reached the foot of College Hill and started to climb. About halfway up, Kerri touched my arm and whispered a warning. "We have company." I started to turn my head but she tightened her grip. "Don't look. There's a half dozen of them following us."

"A half dozen of who?" I whispered back.

"I don't know." Her voice caught and I realized she was frightened. So was I.

"Let's move a little faster."

Three dark shrouded figures stepped out of an alley into our path. Their clothes were shabby and filthy and they moved with an odd gait that seemed furtive, uncertain, but menacing.

"This way!" Kerri hissed the words as she tugged at my arm, drawing me through the gates into the Brown University Quadrangle.

We ran through the darkness, crossed the open space and exited on the opposite side. An oak tree had fallen across the wall and we had to brush its branches aside before getting clear. We hurried along for two blocks, then cut through a parking lot and back onto Angell Street. There were no signs of pursuit.

Which is why we were so surprised when two more tattered figures stepped out from behind a garbage dumpster. Kelly and I froze, then tried to retreat. Someone grabbed me from behind, wrapped wiry arms around my upper body. I heard Kerri shouting as I twisted free, and saw her struggling with two of our assailants. I knocked down the man who'd grabbed me and shrugged off his companion, whose back was twisted into an unusual shape. They attacked silently and with determination, but there was an odd insubstantiality about them, as though they were all half starved. Kerri had already shaken off one of her attackers by the time I reached them, and the other fell silently when I clipped him behind the ear.

We started running, almost directly into the arms of three more, one of whom was carrying a torch. By its flickering light, I saw his face quite clearly, though it was smeared with dirt and sweat.

It was Phil Martin, who lived in Kerri's apartment building, two doors down. At least, it looked like Phil Martin. But the man I'd made small talk with a week earlier didn't have an enormous wen bulging from the side of his neck, and this one did.

We hopped over a low, wrought iron fence and crossed a small, badly maintained lawn. A gate opened onto the opposite side of the block and we emerged cautiously, then turned left. We could hear our pursuers' footsteps but they remained eerily silent, not calling out to one another, not speaking. At the next corner, we spotted another group, half a dozen this time, led by a woman who held a flaming torch in a withered arm that ended with three clawed fingers.

"What's going on?" Kerri's whisper was frantic, near panic.

"Quiet! In here!" We climbed through the shattered window of a gutted store, a copy shop, and crouched behind the counter while they passed. We were both shivering despite the humidity, and shaking with tension.

"What's happened, Danny? What are we going to do?"

I didn't answer until the torch was no longer in sight. then I sat with my back against the counter and searched for calm. "We'll wait here until morning. Once the sun comes up, we'll have a better chance of figuring this thing out."

And that's what we did, dozing fitfully, waking occasionally when some noise penetrated the gloom. Twice I heard what sounded very much like a human scream, but in both cases it was a brief, staccato sound, ended almost as soon as it began. Eventually I fell into a deeper sleep, and when I next stirred, my wristwatch told me it was almost ten o'clock.

But it was still pitch black outside. The sun hadn't risen.

Kerri stirred a few minutes later. "I'm thirsty." Her voice sounded like that of a petulant child.

"I think we should move. Are you ready?"

"I guess so."

We made another effort to reach her apartment, and almost ran into a crowd two blocks short of it. There were at least twenty people sitting in the street, gathered in small groups around a bonfire. Occasionally someone would throw in fresh fuel, pieces of furniture, cardboard boxes, stacks of books. There was enough light to see their faces, and Kerri identified two of her neighbors. One was a hunchback and the other had a club foot.

Neither had been disfigured before now.

Watching from concealment, we noticed that most of them bore some deformity. There was a woman with an oversized head, a man whose spine was twisted into a corkscrew, and another of indeterminate sex was completely bald, skin covered with what appeared to be a dark tattoo. On the far side of the intersection, yet another sat stroking his thighs with something that didn't look at all like an ordinary arm.

We were about to turn away when something changed. Several of the figures stood and began looking around in something close to panic. Kerri's fingers tightened on my arm as the sudden tension reached us, but before I could respond, an enormous black shape erupted from within one of the adjacent buildings.

The bonfire was scattered in the first few seconds, so I didn't see much of what happened clearly, but I would swear that it was an oversized tentacle that attacked those people, people who remained silent even as they died except for one man who gave a prolonged hopeless scream that was abruptly, and terrifyingly truncated. There was a sudden fetid smell in the air so powerful it was palpable. I don't know how many of them escaped, because we turned and ran ourselves, ran back the way we had come. Something deadly had come to Providence.

We kept on until we were short of breath, then ducked into a private residence, fell to the ground in the shelter of some lilac bushes.

Kerri recovered her breath before I did. "What's going on, Danny? What happened to the world while we were underground?" She sounded close to tears.

"I'm not sure that anything happened, Kerri." I sat up. My head spun a few times, then settled down. "I don't think this _is_ the world. Not ours anyway."

"I don't understand."

"Neither do I, but we have to go back."

"Back?"

"Back to the excavation. It's our only chance." But it was a long time before either of us summoned the strength to move. When we started back toward the downtown, my wristwatch indicated it was early afternoon, but the sky said it was midnight.

The darkness was unrelenting. The moon was the most obvious lightsource, but when I looked closely, I couldn't find the familiar features I expected. I wondered if this might be the dark side, if the moon's rotation had changed to expose its hidden face. Even the stars seemed changed; I couldn't find any familiar constellations.

Providence was similarly altered now that I was looking for differences. Some of the buildings were missing, and there was at least one misshapen tower that I'd never seen before.

"If this isn't Providence, then what _is_ it?" Kerri didn't sound like she wanted an adventure any more.

"Another dimension, a parallel universe, a different timeline? Who knows? Something happened here, some incredible catastrophe has altered the rotation of the Earth and moon, maybe changed their orbits. And creatures have arrived on Earth and are hunting down whoever survived the catastrophe."

Kerri stopped in her tracks. "The Old Ones," she said softly.

"What're you talking about?" But I realized what she was implying. "You think Lovecraft came here? That he visited this world and wrote about it?"

"No, not really. But maybe, somehow, he knew about it. I don't know, psychic dreams, clairvoyance maybe. Something like that must have happened."

Maybe.

We made our way down College Hill without seeing another living being. There were fires in the distance, columns of black smoke obscured the stars. The distant hum I'd heard earlier was louder now, and no longer resembled traffic sounds. It sounded organic. We reached the edge of the construction site without incident, although it now seemed evident that there was no construction underway here. The city of Providence was being destroyed in this world, not rebuilt.

I glanced up at the skyline just before it moved.

The unusual building whose shape had been dimly visible before was closer now, and I was staring right at it when the change began. The thin gap of night sky visible between it and the Hospital Trust Tower vanished first, then the upper floors changed shape. And the low rumbling we'd been hearing all night was suddenly louder.

It wasn't a building; it was some kind of gigantic creature.

This time we heard the residents of this dark Providence before we saw them. They were screaming with despair as they poured out of the city, scores, hundreds of them, all desperately leaving their hiding places to flee ahead of this incredible menace. Kerri and I continued forward, desperate to reach the excavation site, but the flood of humanity engulfed us within seconds, clawing their way over torn pavement, shattered buildings, and fallen debris. I was knocked to the ground twice, and Kerri's hand was torn from mine. When I regained my feet, she was gone, and a fresh wave of refugees overwhelmed me as well. Like it or not, I was running back toward College Hill, calling Kerri's name whenever I could draw breath.

Within seconds I was disoriented, but there was a momentary ebb in the stream and I ducked into a doorway, waited breathlessly while the city disgorged more and more of its residents. There must have been thousands of them. Then the darkness grew momentarily more intense, as though something blocked even the pale light of the night sky from the street outside. A final few stragglers raced by and the screaming receded, became more distant.

An hour later, I emerged from my hiding place. There was no other sign of life, and the gigantic shape was nowhere to be seen. I spent the next several hours searching for Kerri, checking each of several dozen dead bodies I encountered, but never calling her name. Even if I'd wanted to, I'm not sure I could have summoned a voice.

Against all the odds, I found her. Stumbled across her, in fact. She was lying behind one of the barricades, so covered with filth I barely recognized her. Blood stained the side of her head and she was unconscious, but her breathing and heartbeat were strong.

I carried her to the tunnel.

The descent was an absolute horror, but nothing compared to what I'd already experienced. I dropped Kerri once and twice we both fell. The second time we slid down the last few meters completely out of control. At the bottom of the slope, I waited long enough to catch my breath, then lifted Kerri over my shoulder and crossed the barrier.

I could never have made it up the other side if Kerri hadn't regained consciousness, partially at least. She moved in a daze, answered my questions in monosyllables, and seemed to have trouble concentrating. I was worried about a concussion, but desperate to confirm that we were back in our own world. By the time we reached the surface, I'd forgotten all my romantic intentions towards Kerri and was swearing at her to keep moving.

Downtown was speckled with electric lights, and a steady stream of traffic moved along the interstate. It was night in this Providence too, but not the same night we'd left. And this one would have an ending.

I brought Kerri to my apartment and left her sleeping on the couch, then flopped onto my bed after shedding most of my filthy garments. As much as I wanted a shower, it would have to wait until morning.

Kerri was still asleep, her breathing easy and regular. I left her undisturbed and took a long, refreshing shower. My head was spinning - I hadn't eaten in almost thirty-six hours - but I had to wash off the residue of our misadventure first. With fresh clothing on my body and a stale donut in it, I touched Kerri's shoulder.

"C'mon, Kerri. Wake up. You need to eat something."

She mumbled something unintelligible and her eyes opened, but they were unfocused.

"Are you okay?" The swelling on her head had subsided and the bleeding had stopped, but I was still concerned about a concussion.

"Dirty." She was staring down at her body, completely covered in dried blood.

"Why don't you take a shower while I fix something to eat?"

She seemed to understand, began unbuttoning her blouse. I felt as though I should turn away, give her some privacy, but the previous day's events were already receding and I felt a fresh awakening of my sexual interest.

I had a moment to realize something was wrong before it happened. Kerri hadn't been wearing a blouse the night before; she'd worn a halter top.

And then the last button was undone and she peeled back the filthy material to release two coiled tentacles from her chest and I fell back in horror, realizing the Kerri I'd rescued from that other Providence was not the one with whom I'd entered it.

THE DUNWICH GATE

I suppose it might have been worse; the engine could have died on some untraveled back road instead of the Massachusetts Turnpike, but there's no such thing as a good place for car trouble, particularly at two in the morning. The state police cruiser pulled up behind me in less than five minutes, and ten minutes after that a contracted tow truck was unwinding the winch cable.

"I don't suppose there are any twenty-four hour repair shops around here." I wasn't even sure where "here" was. The last exit had been for Palmer and Ware, several miles back.

"Hey, guy, there ain't nothing after midnight 'less you go back towards Springfield a good ways." The driver was large and hairy but seemed friendly. "Bert's Garage'll be open tomorrow so I can tow you that far and leave it for morning."

"Is there at least a hotel?"

He barked a short laugh. "Not hardly. There's a motel might have room for you." He chuckled again, a private sound, and turned back to his work.

There wasn't much conversation as we drove off, my car hooked like a fish, using an unmarked service road to leave the interstate. The driver let the truck idle while he unlocked and then relocked the gate. The pavement was cracked and uneven, wound through closely packed trees, emerging onto a narrow rural road that angled sharply away from the highway.

Bert's Garage was tucked between two hills, and it was dark, not even a security light. The weather was unusually warm for late October, almost muggy, and I walked around aimlessly while the driver lowered my car, then climbed back into the cab for the short ride to the Weeping Willow Inn.

I had misgivings about the place, which I suspected offered hourly as well as nightly rates, and the state of the room bore out my suspicions. No television, no telephone, no pictures on the wall, and most definitely no Gideon Bible. But the bed was comfortable and stress related fatigue overcame my reservations and provided me a deep and refreshing sleep.

A phone call the following morning led to reassurances that a mechanic would look at my car first thing. I left the motel's telephone number despite the day clerk's clear expression of annoyance, then asked directions to the nearest diner, since the only food offered by the Weeping Willow Inn was an elderly soda machine.

He reluctantly set down the morning paper, whose headline indicated George Bush was lengthening his lead in the polls over the hapless Dukakis. "Palmer's 'bout six miles down the road."

"Anything closer?" A twelve mile round trip seemed a bit much for coffee and donuts.

"There's a variety store over the Dunnitch line, but you don't want to go there."

"How far is that?"

"Maybe two miles, but there's no road most of the way."

I made him repeat the directions twice so I was sure I understood, then set out.

The sun was high and bright, the air still heavy with moisture. A narrow footpath was visible on the opposite side of a break in the split rail fence just as described, and I followed it through a band of trees, emerging into a field which had clearly not felt the blade of a plow in years. The path curved sharply away, but I picked out the landmark I was looking for, a bald hill, and made my way through light brush that rose to my armpits.

The slope was steep but the lack of vegetation made the climb relatively easy. It was odd how devoid of life the place was. A few trees still stood but their lifelessness was obvious, and I didn't see any grass at all, not even the stain of lichen on exposed rocks. It reminded me of the aftermath of a forest fire, although I saw no charred wood or ash.

The crest was littered with large columns of rock, some of them apparently reshaped by human hands. I suspected that they were at one time standing stones, although none stood today, and spotted a few slabs that were probably lintels. The exertion took its toll and I sat on one of these for several minutes, hoping that the very faint breeze would help dry my sweat soaked shirt. From that vantage point, I noticed a line of pavement in the near distance, close enough to reveal that it was no longer maintained. Presumably this was the old Aylesbury Pike, closed down once the interstate had been completed.

Relatively refreshed, I rose to resume my walk, and in retrospect that's certainly where I made my error. To be fair, the deskclerk had quite clearly said to keep to the lefthand path down the far side of this hill, but I simply took the first one I noticed. It descended rapidly into a buffer of trees so thick that within a few minutes of reaching them, I could no longer see the hill at all.

I emerged onto a dirt road, expecting pavement which I was supposed to follow to the intersection with Dean's Corner Road. Foolishly I assumed my informant had been mistaken and continued, heartened by the sight of a farmhouse off in the distance. When I came closer, I realized it was long abandoned, the windows boarded over, the roof half collapsed, but there was a scattering of other buildings further on and I thought nothing of it.

There were no signs of life, no chickens picking their way around the yards, no dogs barking a warning at my approach, no cows grazing the fields. And no people at all, although these houses were certainly inhabited. I also noticed what I took to be hex signs, elaborate placards mounted on each structure, but lacking the usual variations. There were in fact only two patterns. One was a five pointed star with a flaming eye in its center, the other a churning mass of interlaced strings of color, the latter somehow conveying the impression of coiled tension. Each piece of property bore one or the other, but none mixed the two. It was almost as if they identified two separate factions.   "Republicans and Democrats," I muttered.

At this point, I knew I'd come the wrong way, but I was both too stubborn to go back and too encouraged by the sight of civilization, however deserted.

And then I met Jack Frye.

He saw me before I saw him, although he was sitting out on his porch as plain as day. The house was basically sound as far as I could tell, though the paint was peeling, there were shingles missing from the roof, and weeds had successfully invaded and subdued the yard. One of the star and eye hex signs was displayed prominently beside the front door. Behind the house was the ruined foundation of an even older building, from which the fallen timbers had never been removed but simply allowed to rot.

"You there! Do you stand left of the gate or on the right?"

I stopped where I was, blinking, saw the old man stir from his seat, turned my head.

"Hello! Say, would you mind giving me directions to the center of town. I think I'm lost."

He stood up, stepped forward into the light. A deeply lined face, with a wispy, spadelike beard of white hair. I guessed his age at seventy or more. "Come up here where's I can see you clear."

I stepped over, or rather through, the low picket fence. There were more pickets missing than present. "Is there someplace around here where I can get something to eat?" My stomach was rumbling and I felt lightheaded.

His stare was disconcerting, the eyes intense. "You're not from 'round here."

"No, I'm just stranded while my car is being fixed." Something struck me then. I hadn't seen a single vehicle, moving or parked, since descending from the blasted hill.

"Better come up to the house. No place to wander about this day." He waved me up onto the porch.

I hesitated, but nothing more promising suggested itself. "Do you suppose I could use your telephone?" Maybe I could rent a cab, have someone come pick me up.

The old man opened the screen door with one hand, reached out to grasp my own with the other. "Name's Jack Frye," he said with no warmth. "And I got no phone. Come inside before you're noticed."

Now I've seen enough horror films to know how the next scene is supposed to play, but this was real life, not a movie, and I don't...didn't believe the world held any more surprises for me. Frye was at least twice my age, moved with the slow deliberation of frailty, and I'm not without certain physical resources. So I told myself to stay alert, and allowed him to usher me inside.

It was not what I'd expected. The interior was dark, filled with shadows, but neat and orderly and, insofar as I could tell, clean. Frye was obviously living in the front room; a neatly made bed was tucked into an alcove, flanked by a chest of drawers and a wardrobe. At the opposite end, an enormous oak desk stood against a wall that was covered with documents, newspaper and magazine articles, letters, handwritten notes, a handful of photographs.

"Make yourself t'home and I'll see what's fit to bring out."

I entertained myself with the wall while Frye disappeared into the next room. The very first item I read startled me, an excerpt from a medical study about mental disease in the town of Dunwich, Massachusetts. Dunwich, not Dunnitch; the deskclerk's accent had fooled me. I'd heard of Dunwich before, although my memory refused to provide any concrete information.

Most of the rest of what I read were stories of strange events in the north central part of the state, disappearances, mysterious deaths, cattle mutilations, unexplained noises, UFO sightings, and the like. I was starting to pigeonhole Frye in my mind when I came to what I thought was the clinching bit of evidence, the stimulus for his mental imbalance.

It was a yellowing page from the November 2, 1928 issue of the Arkham Advertiser. The story was a terse but noticeably skeptical account of the tragic disappearance of one Elmer Frye and his family, along with the near total destruction of their house by what was described by neighbors as "an invisible giant". Mention was made of the sole survivor, a son named John who'd sneaked out to visit a friend in Dean's Corners. Was John Jack?

"This is the best I kin do fer ya." Frye had returned so silently I hadn't heard his approach and I started, resisting the impulse to shrink away. He was holding a tray upon which, I suddenly realized, was a cup of black coffee and half a loaf of homemade bread. "Got no butter," he apologized.

It didn't matter. I thanked him and tore off a hunk of the bread, which had a taste rich beyond anything I'd expected. The coffee was good as well.

As my hunger abated, I paid more attention to my surroundings. One wall was dominated by an oversized clock, which I assumed was broken, since it read exactly noon, or perhaps midnight, even though it was barely eleven thirty. Just beneath was a crossbow, clearly an antique though in excellent condition, the stock carved with elaborate symbols, stars and burning eyes predominating. Frye followed my gaze, nodded to himself. "The years are as minutes to them, and their hour is once again at hand."

I stirred nervously, fearing I was about to hear Frye's particular mania, but he fell back into silence.

"I really appreciate this," I told him when I had finished.
"Now if you could just give me some directions back to the motel..."

"I can tell you the way, but I can't guarantee it'll lie still before you."

I had no idea what to make of that, but I kept my face neutral and resolved to pay strict attention to the directions this time. They were simple enough, designed to intersect the road about two miles on the Palmer side of the Weeping Willow. I'd apparently wandered further than I'd thought.

Frye watched me from the porch as I left, turning back the way I'd come, but diverging at a small creek, following it through a field until I reached a gentle swell of ground. From its top, I spotted the split oak with no difficulty, and from there proceeded to the barbed wire fence that led to another dirt road.

Out in the open, I could see the red grain silo that was my next landmark, just beyond a scattering of dilapidated houses. I was supposed to circle around to the right from here, but it was clear that I could save time by following the road's leftward curve. Frye's admonition that I "on no account come within stone's throw of the mill" had struck me as odd at the time, and nonsensical at the moment. My feet were beginning to protest the unusual amount of walking I was doing, and my patience with the entire adventure was wearing precariously thin.

So I turned toward the mill.

The creek I'd followed was one of several outflows from the narrow band of falls which the mill faced, winding through impenetrable woods to my left, trees choked with barberry and sumac and wisteria. It was rather pretty in a chaotic and daunting fashion, and I was paying more attention to the foliage than to my surroundings until I was within a few steps of the mill itself.

The omnipresent hex signs were here as well. The crumbling mill had a particularly large version of the coiled mass, which was reflected on several of the nearby houses. In fact, I could only see one of the stars, and it was quite a distance away, adjacent to the route Frye had suggested I follow.

While I was preoccupied examining the houses, three men stepped out into my path. I didn't see where they'd come from, and there wasn't enough cover to conceal anything larger than a dog between where I stood and the mill, but they'd come silently from somewhere to block my path.

I stopped. Their stance made it quite clear they weren't just watching me pass.

"Could one of you gentlemen give me some directions? I seem to have lost my way." Not entirely true, but I wanted to break the sudden tension.

The silence stretched. Two of the men, those flanking the road, were youngish, barely out of their teens, both wearing coveralls with straps over their shoulders. The one in the middle was older, fortyish, with a thick, full faced beard. All their clothing was dark blue or black, quite full, sleeves down to the wrists, and I was reminded of the Amish.

"On which side of the gate do you abide?"

"I beg your pardon." The older man had spoken, although the words conveyed no meaning to me.

They exchanged looks among themselves before he spoke again. "Is your path to the left or to the right?"

"I don't know where the hell my path lies," I answered intemperately. "I just told you I'm lost. I was hoping you could help me."

"There are many different ways here." His voice was level, unoffended. "If you have not chosen, that favor might be done for you." He half turned his head to the right. "Daniel!"

"Yes, Mr. Bishop?"

"Fetch our guest here up to the barn."

"Wait a minute. I don't have time to sit around here." I backed up a step, warned by something subliminal that the situation was growing more complicated and perhaps even dangerous. "All I want is directions out of your town. If you can't help me, I'll make my own way."

But Daniel was already moving in my direction.

Like I said, I'm pretty rugged physically, and while I don't go looking for fights, I've never shied away from one either. Instinctively I fell into a defensive stance. When Daniel reached for my arm, I slapped his aside, then stepped forward before he could recover and slammed two quick punches into his gut, figuring to discourage him fast and clean.

He staggered a bit, his face slowly registering surprise but no real anger. My hand hurt; he was a lot solider than he looked, and when it was obvious he wasn't going to quit that easily, I decided the rules didn't apply and drove my knee up into his groin.

There was a scream, and I guess it came from Daniel, but he didn't open his mouth to let it out, and I would have sworn the sound came from lower down, from where my knee had buried itself in flesh that was considerably softer than I'd expected. But things are kind of blurry then because one of Daniel's friends had come up on my blindside and something blossomed on the back of my skull and that's the last I remember for a while.

I woke up in some kind of storage room, walls covered with shelves, about a third filled with canning supplies, empty glass jars, sealing rings, a few simple tools mostly rusted past all usefulness. No windows, the door closed. They'd dropped me on the earthen floor but hadn't bothered to tie me up. I was a bit groggy but managed to get to my feet, wondering what in the world I'd gotten myself into.

As yet, I didn't know it wasn't anything in this world at all.

There was a stool in the corner near the door, a long table covered by a tarp pressed against another wall. I tried the door, which was locked, then started looking for something I could use as a weapon. Naturally, I looked under the tarp.

It was Daniel's body, and he was quite dead.

Under other circumstances, I might have felt badly being responsible for a death, but I was too angry and, let's face it, frightened just then to worry about it. The door's hinges were on the inside, but they were so thoroughly rusted in place, I doubt I could have popped the pins even with a hammer and chisel.   So I paced for a while, and sat for another while, and then paced some more, and I was ready to start hammering on the door and screaming when someone opened it.

It was a man I'd never seen before, an albino, his skin chalk white, head bald, perhaps shaved. He gestured for me to come out.

We were in a barn, dimly lit by a few windows set near the ceiling. There were at least a dozen people present, all dressed similarly to the threesome who'd abducted me initially; even the women wore baggy trousers and blouses gathered tightly at wrist, ankle, and throat. At least three were physically deformed, a hunchbacked man, a clubfooted woman, and another man with a disquietingly large lump on his right side, capped by a withered arm.

Most of those present were working at rough tables, painting placards with the serpentine symbol I'd seen earlier, or embroidering it into elaborate banners. No one paid any attention to me except the albino and a second man, fortyish, bearded, unsmiling, who held an elderly but no doubt serviceable shotgun aimed at my midsection.

I decided not to argue when the albino indicated I was to follow him.

They took me to Bishop, the man who'd ordered my abduction, and who now stood with three others, a man and woman in their late thirties, and a teenaged girl, near a fenced off square in the center of the barn. Uncharacteristically, the teenager wore light colored clothing, a simple shift that wasn't much more than a nightgown.

"Would you like to tell me what this is all about?"

Bishop ignored me, waited while the albino fetched a small wicker cage in which was imprisoned a single small bird, a whippoorwill.

"We shall learn if you have been chosen to serve the gate." That remark seemed to be addressed to me, but I had no idea how to respond. Bishop opened the cage and deftly captured the bird, then withdrew his arm. After a moment, the bird flew to my shoulder where it paused a second, then rose swiftly into the air and flew unerringly to one of the open windows and made its escape.

Bishop nodded. "It is well. Two more tumblers fall this day." He turned to the girl. "It is time, Lucy." And to my utter shock, she smiled tentatively and reached down, then removed her shift, standing naked in front of us.

I seemed to be the only one made uncomfortable by that act.

The older woman opened the gate to the pen. Bishop drew a breath, then began to speak. "Yog-Sothoth is the Gate and we are its keys," he declaimed loudly, startling me. "He is the Hand and we are his fingers. Yog-Sothoth is the Gate which is ever ajar, the Night without ending. His touch is glorious and shall transfigure us all. Yog-Sothoth, hear our call."

He kept talking after that, or making sounds anyway. If any of that gibberish had meaning, it was in no language with which I was familiar. Many of the syllables seemed distorted, as though not meant for human tongue and lips, but one phrase was readily distinguishable, and was repeated several times. "N'gai, n'gai, r'kasha nar phtagn."

When he finally finished, or ran out of breath, he nodded to the girl and she stepped forward into the pen.

What followed was so unpleasant, I find it difficult to describe even now. Contrary to what I'd thought, the enclosure was not empty, but whatever waited within was nothing of this earth. Something moved in the air, like a heat shimmer, or a puff of gas. There was the impression of a form, an oversized finger or the head of a snake, or perhaps the tentacle of some deep sea dweller. It was only visible briefly, half visible really; it brushed the girl's right hip, lingered a second, then was gone.

The effect was instantaneous. A web of dark lines spread from the hip across the lower part of her body, as though dye had been injected into the veins. Flesh began to swell around those lines, which grew even darker. Lucy threw her head back in what might have been agony, or perhaps ecstasy, and I recoiled as the ballooning flesh split and reformed within seconds into a new shape, that of some bizarre crab or spider or a blend of the two, with its legs, or its arms, clasped around her torso. It shifted, accompanied by an unpleasant sucking sound, adjusting its position as she turned and came out of the pen.

I'm afraid I had to turn away at that point, trying to control my surging stomach. When I recovered sufficiently to look around, she was wearing dark trousers and a shirt, similar to that worn by the others. But her body was slightly asymmetrical, and I knew what that dark cloth concealed. And wondered about the other malformations I'd seen.

"And now the honor is yours."

I didn't think they'd allow me to decline politely, but as it happened I was spared the effort. The double doors exploded inward in a hail of shattered wood.

We were all caught by surprise, but I had a powerful incentive to recover my wits. Half a dozen men poured in through the wreckage of the explosion, carrying crude weapons, pitchforks, staves, at least one elderly hunting rifle. Within seconds there was a pitched battle underway, the consequences of which I don't know because I took advantage of the confusion to break free and run outside.

It was dusk and I had absolutely no idea where I was, but the appearance of more black clad figures boiling out of the house to my right underlined the necessity to act quickly. I fled into a grove of trees.

Even if I could remember the details of what followed, I wouldn't bore you with them. Suffice it to say I floundered onward, crouching in whatever cover I could find when I heard voices near, as I frequently did, slowing only when fatigue overcame my panic. It was full dark by then, and I had no landmarks to guide me until I reached a small meadow.

There was an opening in the trees, and the risen moon illuminated the crest of a tall hill, a rocky peak looming above a ledge bearing unmistakable shapes. Even from that distance, the silhouette was unmistakable, a circle of standing stones. With no better plan at hand, I set off in that direction.

I was exhausted when I reached the summit, and disheartened to discover that the only lights I could discern from that point were too distant to suggest a reasonable goal. The sky was clear and bright and my surroundings were quite startling. I was approaching my mental and physical limits, decided to rest for a while, but concealed myself in a narrow cleft of rock before closing my eyes and falling asleep.

When I woke, my watch indicated it was nearly midnight. And I was no longer alone.

There must have been at least two hundred people in the clearing below, bearing torches, a handful of flashlights, several score banners and placards with the familiar chaotic swirls of color. I saw no familiar faces, but the clothing was unmistakable. I'd chosen my hiding place well, as it enabled me to watch without being observed in turn.

A stone altar was set within the circle and a figure was standing on it, turned away from me. But when he began to speak, I recognized Bishop's voice immediately.

"It is time to turn the key, to work the lock, to open the gate. The years are as minutes to Them, and Their hour is at hand. N'gai, n'gai, r'kasha nar phtagn. Yog-Sothoth phtagn." I recognized that phrase; Jack Frye had used almost the same words. What was going on here?

Then the earth began to move. No, it didn't move exactly, but there was a sound, a deep formless groaning that felt like motion. I'd experienced earthquakes in Italy and California; this was different.

The assembled cultists, or whatever they were, began stripping off their clothing. Each and every one of them bore some kind of stigmata, some deformity. Either their flesh was warped into odd shapes, extra limbs, grotesque forms, or they were hosts to alien creatures inextricably intertwined with their bodies. I saw tentacles with mouths in the place of sexual organs, scabrous extra arms with the wrong number of fingers, slime covered excrescences on backs, breasts, or elsewhere. Even in the dim light, I saw flashes of color that had never appeared on the human body before. Many of the physical variations were quite beyond description.

Bishop was still haranguing his followers, but now the syllables held no meaning, they were either some foreign language or gibberish or both. Periodically he would pause and they would respond with that now too familiar, and distinctly unsettling phrase, "Ngai, n'gai, r'kasha nar phtagn." Many of the assembled worshippers, as I had no doubt they were, dropped to the ground and began writhing and moaning softly in what I at first thought was the opening moments of a mass orgy.

But from my vantage point, I saw something familiar emerging from the random intertwining of their bodies. They were forming a living representation of the hex sign I'd seen earlier, reproducing the pattern with human and inhuman flesh.

"N'GAI! N'GAI! R'KASHA NAR PHTAGN! YOG-SOTHOTH PHTAGN!" Bishop's voice seemed preternaturally loud, the volume too great to originate in a human throat. The torchlight flickered but I could see quite clearly that he was using no artificial means to amplify his words, but the standing stones, even the ground beneath me, seemed to shake in sympathy.

The opposition attacked then, coming out of the darkness with their primitive weapons, axes, shovels, wooden clubs, a handful of firearms. Several bore pole capped with the star and eye symbol, but these were employed as weapons rather than banners. There was brief chaos around the perimeter of the forming pattern, but Bishop or his followers had anticipated the assault, and previously concealed reinforcements rushed to protect their fellows. I saw bodies fall on both sides, several of whom lay motionless, before the invading force hesitated, then began to retreat.

The ceremony, if that's what it was, continued.

And then there was a sound just behind and above me, and I thought I'd been discovered, could not move, could barely breathe. Bishop seemed to sense that same presence, because he turned toward the summit for the first time, and I saw his face break into an expression of utter surprise as a wooden shaft struck him in the chest, penetrating his heart. A crossbow bolt.

His chant was cut off in mid-phrase, and he fell into the pattern, disrupting it.

I'm not sure exactly what followed. The naked cultists persisted in their efforts for at least several more minutes, but they lacked focus. Heartened, the attackers fought back, and a few even managed to penetrate the fringes of the pattern, kicking out at the recumbent forms, striking them with their weapons.

That's the point where I could stand it no longer. I crept out of the crevice on hands and knees, intent upon escaping this place of madness, but I'd forgotten how slick the rock surface was, overbalanced, and found myself sliding down into the darkness. Then something struck me on the side of the head and when my eyes next opened, the sun was up.

I might have thought it all a dream had I not found torn fabric and broken placards lying scattered about. If anyone had died in the night's battle, the bodies, both human and inhuman, had been removed. Daylight enabled me to locate the Aylesbury Pike, and I walked directly toward it, then followed the cracked pavement until I reached Dean's Corners. The convenience store clerk where I wolfed down coffee and donuts kept a wary eye on me until I left, but no one at the Weeping Willow Inn asked any questions.

I'm back in Managansett now, and my experiences in Dunwich seem almost dreamlike. My research assistant culled the newspaper files and found what I was looking for, a cursory account of unexplained events in that community back in 1928, sixty years ago. Sixty years, sixty minutes. "The years are as hours to them." So we're safe until 2048, I guess.

But what happens then?

THE MANAGANSETT HORROR

"They're breaking through into our world, right here and right now, the creatures you've been writing about, I mean."

"Young man, if you've prevailed upon me to travel all the way out here in service of a practical joke, I warn you that my sense of humor is not at its best at this time of year." The thin, bespectacled man sat back in his chair, trying not to reveal the mild revulsion he felt for his surroundings, which were cluttered and dirty despite his host's evident wealth.

"It's not a joke. How could you think such a thing? You know about them, you've known for years!" There was a glint of desperation, or perhaps madness, in the young man's eyes, and his visitor glanced toward the door, assuring himself there was a direct escape route.

"Listen, Mr. Sheffield, I think my coming here was probably a mistake. You're talking about fictions, fabrications, dark romances extracted from dream landscapes and shared with the reader. They have no basis in reality. I'm flattered that you find them so convincing, but I assure you they are not true."

Sheffield rose from the cane backed chair he'd been sitting in and started pacing from one end of the small room to the other. "Perhaps, sir, you are not aware of the true source of your inspiration. I confess that explanation hadn't occurred to me until this very moment, but you seem sincere and I certainly have no wish to offend a man whose work I have admired for several years. But I have seen the evidence with these very eyes, not dreams but actual manifestations, the first tentative testing of the fabric that separates the universes. And I tell you, sir, I am frightened of the consequences."

His older guest sighed and bowed his head. Howard Phillips Lovecraft was forty five years old, but at that moment he felt as though an additional decade pressed down on his body. It was early January, 1936, the coldest winter he could remember experiencing, and some of the aches in his muscles seemed to have settled in for the duration. It had been much too bitter and inclement to allow him his customary walks around Providence, and perhaps the inactivity had allowed a deeper malady to fester. The sense of confinement continually irritated him, his inability to take any real interest in anything he'd written since "The Shadow Out of Time" had become a major frustration, and now this pointless and unsettling trip to Managansett was threatening to add another layer of unpleasantness to the new year.

"Mr. Sheffield," he said at last. "I have no doubt that you are sincere and well meaning, and I appreciate your having gone to the expense of hiring a car to bring me here. You've given me much to think about. Let me consider the matter overnight and I shall write to you promptly in the morning to apprise you of my thoughts on the matter."

Sheffield stopped halfway across the room, but his head was turned away so that Lovecraft couldn't see his face. "You don't believe me, do you?"

"I didn't say that."

"No, you didn't have to. Do you know, sir, that there is not a single church in all of Managansett?"

"No, I didn't. But it's a very small town, after all."

"Not that small. Name me another community its size in the state, in the country for that matter, that has neither church nor synagogue."

"An interesting idiosyncrasy." Lovecraft made a mental note; there was a promising story lurking in that premise.

"Do you know how many people disappeared under mysterious circumstances in Rhode Island over the course of the last ten years?"

"Certainly not."

"Six hundred and twelve. Of that total, one hundred and thirty two vanished within the town limits of Managansett. Most of them were children. Only ten of these were visitors, transients; the rest were permanent residents."

"Runaways, perhaps. Some victims of unsavory human predators, I imagine."

"Possibly. Have you heard of Monkston's Mound?"

"Of course. A relic of the Narragansett Indians, is it not? Located somewhere in the northern part of your town."

"Yes, it's here, but its origin remains uncertain. Professor Corwin of Brown University has recently completed studies indicating that it preceded the Narragansetts by at least two centuries, probably longer. His findings also include speculation that the mound was the site of human sacrifices designed to propitiate some unidentified entity."

"We're discussing uncivilized savages, Mr. Sheffield. You're obviously an educated man. Surely you understand the difference between illusion and reality."

Sheffield abruptly abandoned his calm demeanor. "I cannot believe this, that I am attempting to convince you, of all people of the truth of what you have written."

"Then perhaps you should consider taking my word for it. I say again, I'm flattered by your attention, but Cthulhu is no more a living, breathing creature than is, say, Sherlock Holmes or Count Dracula."

"Not by that particular nomenclature, perhaps, although his names are legion. I had assumed from the first that you masked reality to avoid attracting attention to yourself. But do you really insist, sir, that you have no personal knowledge of the truth of your own work?"

Lovecraft sighed. "Yes, I'm afraid I do."

There was a long, awkward silence. "Then I fear that I must apologize for wasting your time. The driver will take you back to Providence at your convenience. Please don't feel compelled to offer him a gratuity; he has been more than adequately recompensed for his time."

That was Howard Lovecraft's first intimation that something very odd indeed was happening in the town of Managansett, Rhode Island, and that Paul Alan Sheffield's apparent obsessive delusions were focused on his short stories.

But not his last.

That night, he dreamed of an encounter with a mysterious clergyman in a hidden room within the steeple of the First Congregational Church, among walls filled with ancient books and manuscripts whose arcane subject matter had led to their proscription by clerical and lay authorities alike. It was no surprise to Lovecraft that the clergyman wore Sheffield's face; his dreams were frequently highly colored with details from actual experiences despite their often fantastic nature.

But the following night, he dreamed that he was pursuing a monstrous unspecific menace, a creature of primal evil, across the rooftops of Brown University. He was accompanied in this pursuit by a number of men in medieval dress, all anonymous except for one, Sheffield again.

Lovecraft knew little of Sheffield's personal situation other than his sudden acquisition of a substantial inheritance following the death of his parents. He made some discrete inquiries through a friend of his aunt; anything of a social nature that the Gamwells couldn't learn was probably not worth knowing.

Sheffield, he learned, was in his mid-twenties, a brilliant but taciturn student who had dropped out of Brown shortly before receiving his degree. He had married while still enrolled and was the father of a young boy, although this relationship was moot since the wife had run off six years earlier, taking Paul Junior with her. Sheffield had become even more reclusive following her desertion, and was rarely seen to leave his large but decaying home in Managansett.

January passed away and February took its place, and the strange young man gradually absented himself from Lovecraft's dreams. Desperate for some new direction for his career, Lovecraft reluctantly agreed to collaborate with an old friend, Kenneth Sterling, on an interplanetary adventure, but he lost interest in the project early and only continued out of a sense of obligation. By the first of March, Lovecraft had almost completely forgotten Sheffield.

But Sheffield hadn't forgotten him.

Shortly before noon on March 3, someone knocked on Lovecraft's door. He turned away from the manuscript he'd been working on with considerably less than his usual reluctance; his stomach was upset, a lingering grippe he hadn't been able to throw off. Truthfully, he suspected it was a more serious malady, since he'd suffered the same malaise for several months now. Perhaps in the spring, if the warmer weather didn't bring renewed vigor, he'd consult a physician.

He wasn't expecting a visitor, least of all Paul Alan Sheffield.

"May I come in, Mr. Lovecraft? I promise not to take too much of your time."

No, he thought, you may not come in. But he nodded and swung the door wide.

Sheffield accepted the offer of a seat, shifting the small wooden box he carried so that it lay across his thighs.

"What can I do for you, Mr. Sheffield?"

"You remember our last meeting, I imagine." Lovecraft nodded. "Upon reflection, I understand your skepticism, and I suspect as well that I presented things badly. It's just that I was so certain you already knew at least as much as I, you see. But that's water under the bridge." The younger man shifted nervously in his seat, placed his hands around the two narrowest sides of the box.

"I have brought with me some proof...no, let's say I have some evidence...to support my story. I hope I haven't been too presumptuous in assuming you might grant me the time to explain how I acquired it."

Lovecraft felt a twinge of acidic pain and hastily settled into another chair, facing his uninvited guest. "There are matters I need to attend to, but I suppose a few minutes won't matter." Sheffield seemed much less dangerous in this context, and Lovecraft was frankly relieved at the diversion from his tortured attempt to turn last night's dream of vivisection into a story that would not too closely parallel Mary Shelley's work.

"I mentioned during our earlier encounter that I'd witnessed on several occasions the opening of a breech between the worlds. These visions started during my adolescence, but the incidents were largely benign. I would be granted brief glimpses of bizarre landscapes, clearly not of this plane, with tortured rock formations, deformed vegetation, and sprawling, megalithic buildings obviously not intended for human habitation."

Lovecraft wondered if Sheffield had recently read "At the Mountains of Madness", but held his peace.

"At first, I feared that I was hallucinating, as you might expect. But later, when I realized that some entity on the other side was aware of my presence, I reluctantly accepted the truth of my senses. Managansett occupies a point of intersection, or perhaps just a weakness in the tissue that separates the realities. I'm almost certainly not the first person to observe the preliminary incursions of these dark invasions; I believe I already mentioned to you the frequency with which people disappear within the town limits. The fact that I have evaded them for so long may be simply a matter of good fortune. In any case, I am in obvious need of allies, despite the unwillingness of most people to grant me even so much as a fair hearing. Which is why I have dared to come to you, Mr. Lovecraft."

He'd remained silent, now cleared his throat, wondering what to say. Sheffield was obviously mad, perhaps even dangerously so. Could he be responsible for some of those mysterious disappearances he cited, if in fact the statistics were as he had reported them?

"You mentioned something about proof?"

"Yes, exactly." He moved his hands nervously over the surfaces of the box, finally allowing them to come to rest on a rusty latch attached to the lid. "But first I need to explain how it chanced to fall into my hands."

Lovecraft felt a story coming on, and settled back in his chair, seeking a more comfortable position.

"During the last few weeks, the visions have been stronger, sensory impressions no longer limited to visual. I have heard sounds not meant for human ears, sniffed odors that would make charnel houses seem the finest Parisian perfumeries by comparison. Sometimes these manifestations are spatially limited to a very small area, usually spherical, often no larger than this." He spread his hands about half a meter apart.

"And where exactly to these...manifestations..take place?"

"Here and there. Always within the town limits, of course, but sometimes in the wooded area adjacent to my house, sometimes in the cemetery. Their appearance is clandestine and shortlived, often taking place during darkness, for which reason I believe them to be purposeful rather than mere random events. Something on the other side is directing them, spying out routes of approach, eliminating potential enemies, preparing for more dangerous penetrations at some point in the future. And not too distant a one either."

"And you have no other witnesses?"

"I told you." Sheffield's voice and demeanor betrayed impatience and mild anger, and Lovecraft remembered his earlier concern that the man was mad. "As far as I know, anyone else who has seen what I have has been taken, killed perhaps, or used for whatever inhuman purposes those Others pursue. That's why I was drawn to you; I assumed that you were beyond their reach, that your ability to describe them in detail and in such a public way was proof that you possessed the power to resist them."

"I'm just trying to understand your story, Mr. Sheffield. I meant no criticism."

Sheffield nodded, and his voice softened. "Of course. Please excuse my tone, sir, but I've been under a great deal of stress, as you might imagine. Since our last conversation, there have been two distinct developments which I need to explain to you. They will help you to understand the circumstances through which I obtained this...specimen," and Sheffield tapped the side of the box.

"My frequent exposure to these intrusions has sensitized my mind to their presence, I believe. At least, recently I have begun to anticipate their appearance. Some mysterious inner knowledge guides my footsteps at the appropriate time, and on several occasions I have even been able to see the spatail faults even as they are opening."

"I have already mentioned that the manifestations are of different sizes. Some have been quite large, and yesterday evening I found myself facing one that was adequately spacious to accommodate my entire body. On an impulse, I stepped forward and actually passed between the worlds."

Although he strove to appear impassive, some sign of his true feelings must have been visible because Sheffield flushed and made an impatient gesture.

"I know how all of this must sound, sir, but believe me, I have proof! Once through the barrier, which resisted with no more strength than that of a soap bubble, I found myself free to explore, although as you can well imagine I was unwilling to stray beyond sight of the immaterial portal which had brought me there. The air was chill and dry, but breathable. My body felt unusually light, which I attribute to a difference in gravity between the two planes, but not being scientifically inclined, my observations on the matter are no doubt worthless."

"In any case, I ventured to explore only as far as a nearby, ruined building, built of cyclopean chunks of carved stone. There was no question that it was an artifact; the edges were too even, the layout beneath the chaos a bit too orderly. Not built by men, however. This is hard to describe, but the overall appearance was alien and repellent."

Yes, thought Lovecraft, he's definitely read the novel in Astounding. This might almost be verbal plagiarism.

"I was about to retreat when I realized I was no longer alone. There was something moving just beyond a shattered wall of granite. Using a tilted plinth as a ramp, I climbed high enough to spy on my unexpected companion, who from that distance looked entirely human, although there was something about his gait that seemed a bit out of the usual. Human or not, I had no intention of being caught unprepared, so I turned to descend."

Sheffield let the silence stretch, and Lovecraft broke the tension by offering refreshments. His guest agreed with pathetic eagerness, and waited patiently while his host brewed a pot of tea.

"You were saying?"

Sheffield sipped half a cup of tea before replying. "I turned, planning to make my way back to our world, and found myself face to face with one of the creature's fellows. And 'creatures' is exactly the word I meant. Although human in overall form, its body was unclothed, covered instead with an intricate coating of dark scales fringed with coarse hair. Even that I might have tolerated, but the face! Mr. Lovecraft, the face was something you couldn't imagine in your darkest nightmare!"

"Well, as to that, I've had some pretty dark nightmares myself..."

Sheffield continued, ignoring the interruption. "There were no features such as you'd expect, eyes, nose, mouth. Instead there was a single, muscular tentacle, the length of a man's arm. trifurcated at the very end into three polyps. You can well imagine my horror at finding the thing reaching toward me."

"So I would imagine," he answered drily.

"I threw myself off the plinth, twisting one ankle in the process, and heedless of the pain began running back toward the gateway. Halfway back, I turned to discover a dozen or more of the creatures in pursuit, converging on me from various hiding places among the ruins. I quickened my pace as much as possible, spurred to even greater efforts by the sudden realization that the opening was shrinking visibly. I had only a few seconds to cover the intervening ground or I might have been trapped there!"

"Truly a horrible fate." Madman or not, this Sheffield person was boring as well. A story this derivative would not even have survived a first draft in his earliest days as a writer. But Sheffield seemed oblivious to his words, perhaps to his very presence.

"Just as I threw myself head forward into what remained of the portal, I felt a sharp, fresh pain around my right thigh. Thrown off balance, I failed to guard my head adequately, and when I landed on the ground -- thankfully on this side of the gateway -- I was momentarily knocked senseless."

Momentarily? Lovecraft failed to suppress a thin smile at the thought.

"When I regained consciousness, I found the severed end of one of those crimson tentacles, still fastened around my calf. I removed it, set it inside this container, and made immediate plans to visit you. Surely now that I have proof of my claims, we can be allies against these creatures."

"And you have this...tentacle...with you?"

"Let me show you." As Sheffield fumbled with the catch, Lovecraft stood up. Despite his skepticism, he was curious to see what common object might lie within, confused by Sheffield's paranoia into representing an alien limb.

"Here. You can see for yourself."

And indeed he did. The object was much as Sheffield had described it. He was first reminded of an uncooked beef tongue, for the object was certainly made of muscle tissue. The color was not brilliant enough to qualify as crimson, but it was quite red even for flesh. At one end were three small polyps covered with delicate cilia; the opposite was a torn chunk of fibrous matter.

"I guess the portal closed while it was partway through and amputated it quite close to the base."

Lovecraft extended a tentative finger. It looked moist but was actually dry to the touch. The surface was mildly abrasive, with a hint of stickiness.

"Remarkable," he said softly.

"You believe me now, don't you?"

To cover his confusion, Lovecraft made a noncommittal sound, organizing his thoughts before replying coherently. "Mr. Sheffield, you've certainly brought me food for thought, as well as significant evidence supporting your story. Would it be possible for you to leave this with me for a short time?"

"Certainly, sir." Sheffield stood up and closed the lid, then set the box down on an end table. "I'll return in two days' time if I may, to consult with you further."

"Yes, that will be quite long enough, I would expect." Time enough to confer with someone at the university. Offhand, Lovecraft guessed that Sheffield had brought him part of some obscure but perfectly terrestrial sea creature. But his curiosity was indeed aroused.

"Then I shall take up no more of your valuable time, Mr. Lovecraft." And a moment later, Sheffield was gone.

But two hours later, when Lovecraft prepared to set out on a ten block walk to keep his appointment with Professor Arthur Blodgett of Brown's oceanography department, he discovered that the box was empty, bearing no trace whatsoever of its former contents.

Lovecraft's final encounter with Paul Alan Sheffield occurred thirteen days later. Sheffield did not keep his scheduled appointment, his telephone had long since been disconnected, and he failed to respond to two letters. For his part, Lovecraft couldn't get the incident out of his mind, conscious or subconscious. He was unable to work when awake, trying instead to decide whether he'd been fooled by the power of suggestion, an illusionist's trick, or whether there was indeed some unearthly influence at work. At night, he was unable to rest, his sleep troubled by nightmarish visions.

In one recurring dream, he found himself inside his old quarters at 598 Angell Street. The house had changed dramatically, its beams sagging, carpets and walls coated with mold, filth lying in thick layers on every surface. Then he would hear Sheffield's voice calling from somewhere in the house, but whenever he investigated, he would instead find a vaguely humanoid creature with a single tentacle where one would normally expect to find a face.

The other dream occurred only once, on the night before he finally heard from Sheffield. In this dream, he'd been attacked by a horde of brightly shining insects which burrowed through his skull and into his brain, implanting there various images of alien landscapes, scenes filled with crumbling ruins, stunted vegetation, and vaguely perceived creatures moving at the periphery of his mind's field of vision.

Then came the message, late on the thirteenth day.

"I've been to the other side again, Mr. Lovecraft, and I became disoriented and lost. Have only now found my way back. Please come to my house at your earliest possible convenience and I will show you the way. Polks is holding a car for you."

It was signed "Sheffield" and had been delivered by a private courier.

A terse call confirmed that Polks Rental Agency indeed had a vehicle reserved in Lovecraft's name. "Whenever you want 'er, sir, she's ready to go."

Without a moment's hesitation, he called for it to be sent immediately, then quickly stepped next door to borrow a certain item from his neighbor, Mr. Harrison, a retired police sergeant. When the car arrived, Lovecraft was so lost in thought that he almost failed to answer the man's knock.

The sun dropped below the horizon before they reached Managansett.

Sheffield opened the door before Lovecraft could ring the bell, had evidently been waiting, watching for his arrival.

"Come right in, sir. I have so much to tell you, I hardly know where to start."

Although he'd experienced second thoughts during the long ride out from the city along Route 13, Lovecraft discovered the need to understand what was going on had surpassed even fears for his own survival, whether the danger came from inhuman invaders dwelling in another realm or simply a particularly convincing and clever maniac.

"You implied you had something to show me? That you know the way between the worlds?"

"Yes. Yes, in fact, I do." For a moment, Sheffield looked inordinately smug. "My mind is attuned to them now. I can sense the gateways before they open."

"And do you anticipate their appearance in the near future?"

"Within minutes, now that you ask. And conveniently close at hand."

"And where might that be?"

"In the cemetery, just across the way." Sheffield nodded toward the front of the house. "They manifest themselves there quite frequently. Do you truly wish to see? There's a certain degree of danger, you realize."

"Yes, I do."

It was still quite cold outside, and there was a bitter wind that had blown in with the fall of darkness.

The two men walked briskly from the Sheffield property, across the ill maintained roadway, and through a small and largely overgrown field until they reached the unlocked gate of the town cemetery. Even in the darkness, Lovecraft was impressed with its size and accouterments. From what he could see, it rivalled Swan Point Cemetery in Providence, despite being located in a small, rural community.

Sheffield led the way silently along winding paths, passing markers that varied from simple stones to elaborate statues, fenced family plots, and a handful of large mausoleums. It was to one of these last that he found himself escorted.

"Through here." Ahead was a wrought iron gate, slightly ajar.

"Are you quite certain?" It was ludicrous, he realized, to be hesitating at a minor intrusion into the sanctity of someone's private burial place, when faced with the certainty that he was dealing with either alien creatures or a purely terrestrial madman.

"It's quite all right. As a matter of fact, this is the Nicholson vault, my mother's family. And I'm the last in her line. Don't be afraid. I took the liberty of coming over earlier to turn on the gaslights inside."

Lovecraft thought of Poe and Usher and shivered slightly, not because of the cold air.

The interior of the vault was nondescript, much as he expected, though surprisingly neat and orderly. Cleaner than Sheffield's house, he realized.

"This is the place?"

"Right here. Somewhere near the far wall. Just be patient for a moment." There was something new in Sheffield's voice. The uncertainty and weakness were gone, replaced by self-confidence that verged on bravado. Lovecraft glanced sideways, saw the man's face twisted into an expression of complete triumph. "It's starting right now."

And indeed something peculiar was happening. Lovecraft felt it in the air, a tension that was absolutely physical. Then a faint odor reminiscent of charred wood. He turned toward his companion, about to ask a further question, and realized that something else was moving in the vault.

At first, Lovecraft thought he'd dreamed the entire day's events, because what he saw now was an echo of his previous night's dreams. A horde of luminescent insects seemed to materialize out of empty space, hovering briefly before moving in unison toward a human brain. But it wasn't his brain they sought, but rather that of Paul Alan Sheffield, burrowing through his skull and disappearing within so quickly that Lovecraft couldn't even cry out a warning.

Which might have been superfluous in any case. Sheffield appeared unaffected, continued to smile smugly. "Here it comes now."

A small glowing sphere appeared at the far end of the room, hovering at eye level for a few seconds, then rapidly expanding to completely obscure the opposite wall.

A magnificent vista was revealed within the framework of the sphere. On the far horizon, a misshapen castle was backlit by shivering lightning strikes which seemed to originate at ground level and spear upward into the sky. Nearer at hand, several smaller buildings were scattered across a landscape that reminded him of a painting by Hieronymus Bosch, except that there was animation here. The fleshy, spatulate leaves on the twisted trees moved gently, as though disturbed by a breeze. Centipedelike creatures with scores of legs flowed across the landscape everywhere except in the immediate vicinity of one of the smaller buildings, the only one that appeared relatively intact.

"What is it?" he whispered. "What does it all mean?"

"Just watch." Sheffield was staring directly into the sphere, fully engaged now. His expression was intense and almost joyful, reminding Lovecraft of certain religious orders who flagellated their bodies until they hallucinated visions of redemption.

And then something immense moved, emerging from behind the singular building, something that Lovecraft almost recognized as a child of his own imagination. Its body was without specific form, but there were tentacles and claws and other limbs and orifices that defied description. And it seemed to be moving directly toward them, aware of their presence.

"Lord Cthulhu is coming for us," breathed Sheffield, caught up in some strange private ecstasy.

As more and more of the immense creature emerged, Lovecraft forced himself to look away. It was so loathsome, his already touchy stomach was threatening to rebel entirely. When he did so, he became fully apprised of the state of his companion for the first time since the manifestation began.

Sheffield was delighted.

"You're enjoying this, aren't you?"

Without turning his head, Sheffield nodded. "My power has been growing and now, finally, I can keep the door open long enough for Lord Cthulhu to cross over. As his chief chronicler here, I thought it only fair that you be present to witness his return to the world he once ruled."

"But I made Cthulhu up, you idiot! Whatever this is, it's not what you think."

"You're wrong, Mr. Lovecraft. It's exactly what I think."

And in that instant, Lovecraft knew that Sheffield was right. Conquering his revulsion for violence, he extracted Mr. Harrison's revolver from his pocket and fired it a single time. Sheffield turned with an almost comical look of surprise on his face.

"You can't stop them. You haven't the power." And then he fell with such an air of finality that Lovecraft knew even before he checked that the man was dead.

The vista of another world and all that it contained blinked and was gone in the same second.

"The mind is a powerful thing, Mr. Sheffield." He stood over the body of the man he'd killed, reassured by the sound of his own voice. "But some minds are creative and some are destructive. Yours was the latter. You didn't witness these manifestations, you caused them. The wave of disappearances in Managansett started immediately after your wife and son deserted you, so you found a way to punish everyone else, by taking away their loved ones, dumping them into some ethereal other world that was entirely a product of your warped mind."

He replaced the revolver in his pocket and began extinguishing the gaslights. "Since you lacked the ability to be genuinely creative, you borrowed concepts from my stories to give shape to your revenge. But the one thing you lacked was public recognition, and who better to acknowledge your success than your unwitting collaborator? You turned the children of my imagination into a deadly peril, and for that, among many reasons, you deserved to perish."

With some effort, Lovecraft managed to resecure the lock on the gate. The ground had not thawed enough to accept footprints and with any luck, when Sheffield's disappearance was finally noticed, no one would think to look here.

The driver returned Lovecraft to Providence, where he resumed writing intermittently in the months that remained to him, but never with the enthusiasm that had once powered his work. He was too well aware of the possibility that someone else might pervert his vision in the future.

And too fearful that his imagination might give form to some other talented madman's destructive impulses.

NIGHT DUTY

When Joan told me she was going to have to go tend to her sick uncle for a few days, I almost welcomed the prospect of a break. Don't get me wrong; I loved Joan very much and I was on the verge of asking her to change her name from Trumbull to Sheffield. But as it became clearer to me that this was the woman I wanted to marry, I began to have doubts about my resolve, and I wanted a breather to think things through. I'm basically a quitter, have been all my life. I dropped out of college, twice, and jilted my first fiancé two days before the wedding. When Joan and I met, I was twenty seven, had held six jobs in four different fields, and was currently in the process of breaking the lease on my apartment. She was twenty two and her first novel had just been knocked off the *New York Times* bestseller list after a six week stay.

"Want me to come along?" I asked insincerely.

She shook her head, throwing clothes apparently at random into her suitcase. "Not necessary, Peter. I shouldn't be more than a week or so."

"I didn't even know you had an uncle."

"Ethan's kind of the black sheep. Never leaves Crayport. We visited him maybe four or five times when I was a kid. Duty visits. It was Dad's home town, but I don't think he liked it there much. Can't say I blame him. He was Dad's brother, but you'd never have guessed it. Entirely different people."

"What is it, an old industrial town?'

"Nope. Fishing village mostly. On the rotted side of picturesque. Uncle Ethan doesn't even have a telephone."

"So I can't check up on you."

"Fraid not. First drunken orgy is scheduled for Tuesday."

"Just don't run off with some sexy fisherman." I interrupted her packing for a quick kiss and hug.

"No fear. I get sea sick watching boats from shore and I don't eat fish. Besides, where would I find another man with eyes like yours?" This last was a reference to my eye color, the left one green, the right blue. All of the men in my family share the trait.

"I promise not to let the apartment get too messy while you're gone."

"Yeah, right," she answered sarcastically, and resumed packing.

Long before the first week ended, I missed her so deeply that my doubts were well and truly dispelled. I wrote her a long, sloppy letter, then didn't mail it because I figured she'd be back before it reached Crayport. A week later, it still lay on the night table on Joan's side of the bed. She hadn't returned.

I sent a telegram. No answer.

I'd been working as assistant manager at a variety store just outside Baltimore for the past year, almost a record for me. I told my boss I needed a couple of days off, over the weekend maybe, for some personal business. She told me I couldn't be spared. I explained that it was really an emergency and that I could shift the days to whatever caused the least inconvenience. She insisted that this was the height of the tourist season and I couldn't be spared.

Scratch another career opportunity.

I parked our canary with a neighbor, packed up a suitcase almost at random - Joan and I were a good match on that issue. The Ford wasn't pretty but it was reliable. Route 95 almost all the way. Exited north of Boston and promptly got lost. Ended up in a generically scenic town where no one was particularly helpful but eventually got directions to Crayport, which led me to one of the worst maintained roads I've ever encountered. There were potholes inside some of the potholes, the pavement was completely worn away in spots, and it was clear that the frost heaves from the previous winter had never been repaired. The road wound its way endlessly through deserted farmland and wooded areas, eventually sloping down toward what I realized was the ocean.

Crayport lunged out from behind a hill and confronted me. That's the only way I can describe it. One second there wasn't a human made object within sight; the next I was bumping and juttering toward civilization. How can I describe my initial impression? The words I'd use to describe most New England fishing villages would be "clustered along the shore", "nestled among the hills", or perhaps "scattered among the dunes". Crayport crouched warily beneath some impressive cliffs to the north and glared as I approached.

I've vacationed and sailed along the shore between New Haven and Mount Desert Island several times with my parents and twice with parties my own age. Never before had I seen such an unpleasant looking community. None of the buildings, judged individually, were particularly ugly, although they shared a tendency toward dilapidation and decay that seemed as much a product of neglect as of the corrosive ocean air. Assembled as they were, however, the town looked more than slightly odd. Structures had been erected at odd angles along streets that turned and twisted without obvious purpose. Many of the small, ill tended plots of land were decorated with stone statues that reminded me of the ubiquitous porcelain madonnas of New Bedford, though these weren't remotely human in appearance. As I approached the center of town, the buildings to either side crowded upon and occasionally even overhung the narrow passages. I was forced to slow to a crawl because turns would be completely disguised until I actually reached them.

Few of the stores had signs, and most were dark inside, although I occasionally saw pedestrians enter or leave. There were quite a few people about, but each seemed to be preoccupied with his or her own thoughts. I didn't see a single head turn in my direction, even though I passed only two other moving vehicles during the first ten minutes I spent in Crayport. The women seemed inordinately fond of shawls, reminding me of the Portuguese market in Fall River where I'd worked for a summer. The sunny day had turned overcast and the ocean was gray flecked with whitecaps.

I was hoping to find a post office or police station, because Ethan Trumbull's address was simply Trumbull House, Crayport. There was no sign of either on the main street, which ended abruptly at an even less well maintained frontage road that provided access to the town wharf. To the north, the road was clearly no longer in use and probably impassable, even though it led toward a stretch of impressive cliffs. To the south, it disappeared almost immediately behind a deserted open air marketplace. I pulled over to the curb and parked, intending to walk back into the commercial district and ask for directions.

The stink assaulted me as soon as I stepped out of my air conditioned car. There was salt in it, of course, and hints of dead fish, although from where I stood, it seemed unlikely that any of the moored vessels below were still functioning. They wore coats of rust, peeled paint, layered barnacles, and general decay even worse than I'd seen in the town itself. There were dark clusters on the narrow beach that were probably piles of rotting seaweed, and in fact I saw clumps of mottled yellow and green vegetation scattered along the sidewalk. Stains of moss decorated some of the buildings and grotesquely undisciplined vines strangled many of the trees.

My eyes stopped tearing after a minute and I started walking briskly back toward the intersection where I'd noticed a variety store. A woman emerged from the building across the street - no sign on the door - but she froze at the entranceway when she saw me, then retreated inside. Feeling very much the intruder, I marched determinedly to my destination and entered.

Superficially, it looked very much like an ordinary convenience store. Narrow aisles with small quantities of name brand necessities. A row of glass fronted coolers along the rear wall. Cigarettes and candy bars at the register. There were no customers, and for a moment I thought I was alone. Then an acne scarred youngster stood up from behind the counter and glanced in my direction.

"Hi. Could you tell me how to find Trumbull House?"

The clerk stared at me blankly.

"Is there a police station or post office nearby where I could ask?"

"No post office." Speaking seemed to cause the man pain. He glanced at the cash register meaningfully.

I took the hint. "Give me a pack of those," I said, pointing at a pyramid of cigarettes. He took my money and I pocketed my purchase, wondering why I'd chosen them. I don't smoke.

"I really need to find Trumbull House," I said as firmly as I could.

"Try the south end." And before I could ask further, the clerk sat down and picked up a pornographic magazine, pointedly dismissing me.

The south end of Crayport was, if anything, even more depressing than the rest of the town. The buildings had broken windows, a collapsed roof here and there, yards full of trash and weeds and derelict vehicles. And those were the occupied houses. No street signs, of course, and the few mailboxes were universally nameless. Fortunately I spotted Joan's bright red Saab parked snugly up against the side of one of the larger houses.

There was no driveway so I pulled in alongside her car and parked on a patch of reasonably white sand. The house was two stories tall with a widow's walk at its crest, though most of the railing for that was long gone. The windows were all shuttered and I might have believed the place deserted if it hadn't been for the car and a wire mesh pen full of chickens that filled most of the small backyard. Trumbull House had been built right on the shore, and its far side was connected to a small, private pier where I could see two small boats bobbing on the lapping waves. Both had oar locks, but one was fitted with what appeared to be a small mast.

The cry of seagulls had accompanied me ever since I'd arrived, and they'd been hovering overhead whenever I was out of my car. Not so here. They wheeled away from Trumbull House so abruptly that it caught my attention. I didn't blame them particularly.

The place didn't look particularly inviting. The Saab was covered with a thin layer of salt and dust and two of the tires were flat. Some of the chickens regarded me dolefully, but the rest continued pecking at invisible treats on the ground.

There was no doorbell, so I knocked on the front door. Several times. I had just about decided that no one was home when I heard a stirring inside and then the sound of a latch being undone. The door opened and a wizened, unattractive woman blinked at me.

"Joan?" My voice must have betrayed how I felt.

"That bad, huh? Come on in, Peter. I was wondering if you were going to show up." I winced silently when I realized that she had used "if" rather than "when", but accepted her invitation.

The front room of Trumbull House was no more prepossessing than the exterior. Fortunately, the shuttered windows kept out most of the daylight and I couldn't see how dirty and disorderly it really was.

"How's your uncle?"

Her eyes flickered to the ceiling and back. "Dying, I think. The doctor tries to sound positive but he doesn't try very hard."

"Wouldn't he do better in a hospital?"

"Maybe." She didn't sound enthusiastic.

"And how have you been?"

"I'm all right, appearances notwithstanding. Just tired is all. I was up very late last night. Come into the kitchen; I'll make us some coffee."

I'll spare you a description of the rest of the house, particularly the kitchen, which would have thrown a health inspector into cardiac arrest. Joan got back some of her color with the coffee, even showed traces of her old liveliness. But I could tell she was exhausted, dispirited, and possibly even ill herself.

"How long did you plan to stay?"

"As long as necessary," I answered.

"But your job . . ."

I waved it away. "Wasn't a very good one. Besides, I couldn't leave you alone with all this."

"It might have been better if you had," she almost whispered, then shook her head. "Sorry, feeling sorry for myself. I do appreciate your coming, Peter, but you shouldn't have quit your job. It looks like this could drag on for some time. Uncle Ethan might last for weeks, or even months, and then there are other obligations I need to attend to."

"What kind of a boyfriend would I be if I left you to deal with this alone?"

"A sensible one," she said softly. And I must have looked as offended as I felt because her face softened and she laughed self consciously. "I'm just tired and feeling sorry for myself. Why don't you bring your stuff inside? At least we have a king sized bed to sleep in."

Ethan Trumbull was almost semi-conscious so our introduction was one-sided. His room smelled like death - disinfectant mixed with decades of dust, mold, and other even less savory aromas. Joan dealt with his bedpan, checked his pulse, and performed other arcane rites while I unpacked my suitcase into a dresser in the only room she'd cleaned to something remotely resembling her usual standards. She hadn't made up the bed, but the sheets were crisp and white.

When she joined me we talked for a while, then used the bed for a while, then talked some more. Joan grew more animated as the afternoon edged toward dusk, but she was clearly exhausted, physically and emotionally, and troubled more deeply than I'd expected. Her uncle was dying, of course, but they'd never been close, and I could sense that she was acting out of duty rather than affection. Nevertheless, something was profoundly depressing her, and she deflected every attempt I made to find out what was wrong.

I offered to take her out for supper, but she insisted on cooking a meal at the house. I was not overjoyed at the prospect of eating food prepared in that kitchen, but she was determined and eventually produced a very satisfying casserole. Her uncle had soup in his room, which she spoon fed to him after we'd finished our own meal.

"He only recognizes me some of the time now," she told me later. "He'll be reasonably lucid for a day or two, then drop out of it for the next couple."

We used the bed again, and then eventually fell asleep in it.

I woke up just before midnight and found myself alone. I lay there for a few minutes, listening to the night sounds, the house settling noisily, the distant cry of gulls, waves breaking along the shore. Then I heard a door open and close, and footsteps on the boardwalk down to the pier which ran right under the bedroom window.

A vague sense of wrongness prodded me out of bed and over to the window. I was just in time to see Joan, fully dressed, disappear into the darkness. She was carrying a burlap sack over her shoulder, and I could have sworn that the sack moved of its own volition. Then she was beyond the light. I fretted, wondering if I should get dressed and follow. I was still being indecisive about it when there was the flicker of flame, then a steady glow. It was an oil lantern, which illuminated Joan as she stood unsteadily in one of the two small boats, the masted one. There was no sail on the mast, which served instead as a support for the lantern. She took up the oars and a minute later Joan, who claimed she occasionally became sea sick in the bathtub, passed beyond my field of vision, rowing steadily toward the open sea.

She was gone for almost three hours.

I can't say I waited intently because I dozed off more than once, leaning against the window frame. But I was awake when the bobbing lantern reappeared, watched as she moored the small boat, extinguished the light, and came ashore. The burlap was empty now, lay loosely over her shoulder. When she returned to the bedroom, I was back in place, pretending to be asleep. I wasn't sure how to deal with this new development, and didn't want to confront it unprepared.

She said nothing about her excursion the following morning, but after checking on her uncle, she returned to bed and slept until noon.

I explored Trumbull House while she was asleep, with particular attention to the pier. I couldn't find anything unusual about the boats. The lantern was in a small wooden cabinet mounted on one of the supporting timbers, along with a supply of oil and wicks. Fresh feed had been scattered for the chickens, who were disposing of it with enthusiasm. I found the burlap sack, empty, on a shelf in the shack adjacent to their enclosure. In the house itself I could ferret out nothing of interest. There were no books, no magazines, no personal papers that I could discover. There was no television, no stereo, no tape deck, and no radio. In fact, there was almost nothing that I would consider a personal effect at all. It was as if Trumbull House was a rental place that had fallen into disuse and decay.

Joan eventually appeared, dressed in a sweatshirt and jeans that clashed, her hair only half combed, and announced her intention of making some lunch. A few minutes later she was disproportionately upset about having found nothing left to eat. "There's a grocery store back in town," I said unnecessarily. "We could do a shopping run."

"Yes, of course," she answered distractedly.

She would have walked there and back if I hadn't suggested using the Ford.

The grocery store actually had a sign, which read "Groceries". There were three other customers inside when we entered. The first, an elderly woman, glanced pointedly out the window and ignored us. Clearly she didn't care for outsiders. The other two customers glanced at us warily but neither acknowledged our presence by so much as a nod, nor did the clerk, who retreated behind her counter and began unnecessarily rearranging the candy rack.

Joan went up and down the aisles quickly, selecting items almost at random. I had never known her to venture into a grocery store without a carefully planned list. In less than five minutes, we had filled two of those small plastic baskets the stores provide. Apparently satisfied, Joan led me to the front, then turned abruptly and stepped outside, still carrying the basket. I stopped, confused and momentarily frightened, but the clerk pointedly looked away.

When she realized I hadn't followed, Joan stopped. "Come on, Peter. We have everything we need."

"But . . ." I glanced helplessly toward the clerk, whose back was now stoically presented to me.

"Come on!" she insisted and, confused and dismayed, I did so, feeling like a shoplifter.

"But we haven't paid for any of this!" I protested.

Her face was motionless for a few seconds, then sketched a smile. "They'll put it on my uncle's account. Don't worry about it."

"But how will they know how much to charge? They didn't ring it up."

"I'll send them a list later on. This is a small town. People trust one another to do their duty." And she laughed then, but it was without humor and did nothing to make me feel better.

Back in the Ford, I turned down a side street to reverse direction and saw what, to my surprise, appeared to be a fairly modern, brightly lit diner. It even had a sign: Nathan's Place. Impulsively, I pulled over to the curb and killed the engine.

"Let's have lunch before we go back."

Joan's face displayed what I could only describe as acute distress. "I'd rather not. It looks like a dive."

"I've eaten in worse. Come on." I opened my door.

"Really, Peter, we shouldn't leave my uncle alone."

I refrained from pointing out that she'd deserted him for at least three hours the previous night. "We won't be long. It'll do you good to eat someone else's cooking for a while, even if it is greasy and full of MSG."

She was still protesting when I opened her door and took her arm, but eventually she accepted the inevitable and let me lead her inside.

There was a sudden, palpable, uncomfortable silence when we entered the diner. No one turned to look in our direction, not even the waitress. We seated ourselves and waited until, feeling stubborn as well as offended, I went to the counter and asked for some service. She took our order without smiling and eventually returned with our food, which was as Joan had predicted, greasy and undercooked. When we had finished, Joan started to get up.

"We don't have the bill yet," I told her.

"They'll put it on my uncle's account."

"No they won't!" I was starting to get actively annoyed now. "This is my treat, such as it is, not your uncle's."

It took a few more minutes to get our check, which came only after I waved down our waitress again. It was about half what I expected and I read the detail. She'd charged me for what I'd ordered but for none of Joan's meal.

"Wait here," I told Joan and cornered the waitress in the condiment cubicle.

"We're having a two for one sale," she told me with absolutely no warmth. "One person gets to eat free."

I didn't believe her, but it wasn't worth arguing. Instead I collected Joan, perversely left the waitress a tip equal to the cost of Joan's meal, and paid the cashier. He didn't say a word and never met my eyes.

That night, I was already awake when Joan quietly rose from the bed, collected some clothes, and slipped out of the room. I waited until I heard her go downstairs, then got up as well, slipped into a sweatshirt and jeans, and waited. The outside door opened and closed. A few minutes passed before she appeared outside the window, carrying the burlap sack, hastening toward the pier. I waited until she had the lantern lit before following. By the time I reached the pier, she was gone, but the elevated lantern was an adequate beacon. I untied the second boat, seated myself at the oars, and prepared to follow.

Rowing isn't as easy as it appears. Within ten minutes my arms were beginning to ache, and I wondered how Joan was managing. But somehow she did, even gained some distance, although the lantern was never completely out of sight. After three quarters of an hour I was ready to quit, and in fact stopped for a while to rest, even though that caused my stressed muscles to knot. I was reluctantly preparing to resume rowing when I noticed that the lantern light hadn't receded. I thought at first that Joan was resting as well, but as the minutes passed, I realized that this was as far out as she was planning to venture.

Time passed slowly. There was a cold breeze sweeping over the water that cut right through my clothing. The salt air held an unpleasant tang that grew stronger over time, as though shoals of rotting seaweed were drifting toward us from upwind. I think I slept for a while, because I was wakened by a single, short lived cry that I couldn't identify. Not a gull certainly, and not human either. A human voice spoke then, so distant that I couldn't make out the words, which continued for less than half a minute. Then came a thrashing of waves that lasted a few seconds before subsiding. I blinked, trying to pierce the darkness, but to no avail.

A moment later I heard the sound of oars and realized Joan was on the move again. I hesitated until I was sure the lantern was moving toward shore, then bent to the task, determined to get back and moored before she arrived.

It was a close race. By the time I reached the bedroom window, the lantern was already moving on the pier. I shucked off my clothes and climbed under the blankets, hoping to generate enough body heat to disguise my excursion. When Joan returned to bed, she said nothing, and perhaps she was fooled. But I don't think so.

It was well after noon before she stirred herself the next day. By then I had already turned the burlap bag inside out and confirmed my suspicion. There were feathers in it. There were too many chickens to count, but I suspected that there'd been one more the day before, and yet another the day before that, and so on.

When Joan came downstairs I offered to make lunch, but she waved me off and disappeared into the kitchen. She emerged a little later with an unruly but edible salad. I let her finish eating before dropping the bomb.

"Care to tell me what you were doing out on the ocean last night?"

Her face didn't change, and she didn't answer right away. I think she'd orchestrated her explanation well in advance, but still wasn't sure how it would play. "I was doing what's necessary."

"Necessary? Necessary to whom? And for what?"

I waited patiently and she finally answered. "The Trumbull family has an obligation to Crayport. It was a duty my uncle filled until his illness, and my grandfather before him. It's a, well, a kind of superstition."

"What, are you propitiating an ocean spirit or something? Do you sacrifice a chicken every night to protect the town from evil?" I meant it as a joke, but Joan's response was without humor.

"Yes, more or less."

I sighed. "Joan, you don't believe this nonsense, do you?"

She matched my sigh. "The town believes it. That's why they won't accept my money, you know. In exchange for performing the ritual, the Warder is given whatever he, or she, needs."

"And if your uncle dies, then you take his place, is that it?"

She nodded, then looked away, her eyes suddenly full of pain. "I can't just walk away from this, Peter."

I squirmed impatiently. "Look, Joan, this is just a stupid superstition. You said that yourself. If the local people believe in some ridiculous nonsense, that's their problem, not yours. Let them deal with it."

Joan shook her head. "It's more complicated than that, Peter. You don't understand."

She was right; I didn't. And I would have said so except that I could tell by the set of her shoulders that she'd slipped into one of her stolidly stubborn moods. Clenching my fists, I tried to project a calm I didn't feel. "I'm going for a walk. We'll talk about this later."

"It won't do any good," she said softly, but I was already heading for the door.

I walked rather than drove back into Crayport proper, and by the time I reached those cramped, dingy streets, I'd regained an icy sort of equilibrium. And I had a plan. I visited the local drug store - no sign - and the liquor store - also no sign, then trudged back to the south end. Joan was feeding the chickens.

We didn't talk at all before supper, and by then the sun had already dropped behind the western hills. As Joan dished out the goulash, I revealed my secret.

"God, yes," she breathed at me. "What a great idea."

I poured a generous helping of ginger brandy into a glass and handed it to her, then a smaller portion for myself. This was Joan's weakness, I knew. We'd ended up in bed for the very first time after opening - and finishing - a bottle together. Fortunately, she'd felt the same way sober.

By the time I was pouring her a refill, she was a lot closer to the old Joan than she'd been since I'd arrived, and I was tempted to revive our argument. Instead, I decided to stick to my original plan.

I surreptitiously dropped the sleeping tablets into her drink, waited for them to dissolve before offering it to her. Yes, I know how bad that sounds, but I was convinced that if she could spend just one night sleeping through, particularly when nothing bad happened as a consequence, it would banish her obsession and restore the old Joan.

Halfway through the third brandy, she dozed off. I carried her to the bedroom, undressed her, and checked on Uncle Ethan, who had still not reacted to my presence in the house. It was dark by then and I prowled restlessly, anxious to have the night over with and the crisis resolved. Finally I went to bed, suspecting I wouldn't be able to sleep well, and I was right. Just before midnight, I woke up in a cold sweat, convinced that Joan had somehow thrown off the effects of the drug and wandered off as before.

But she hadn't. Her breathing was deep and regular.

I couldn't get back to sleep, a conclusion I accepted after a half hour of tossing and turning. Eventually I grew concerned that my restlessness would waken Joan, so I rose quietly, dressed and tiptoed downstairs. The night smell was less overpowering than usual, so I went outside, planning to stroll around the property, ending up instead on the road to town.

It was deserted. No surprise that. Half the streetlights were out and the other half did little to dispel the gloom. The town was so depressing that I turned instead toward the wharf, where the dozen or so fishing vessels remained moored. Since arriving in Crayport, I had yet to see even one of these weigh anchor.

I was sitting on the very end of the wharf, staring out to sea, when the change started. First came the stink. It was the rotted seaweed all over again, raised to the nth power. The foul miasma was so thickly fetid that I scrambled to my feet and half ran back toward shore. The stench followed me, rolling over the waves, then the beach. About the same time I noticed a prickly sensation in the air, as though particularly violent lightning was on its way. Then the sound of the surf changed, grew more violent and less regular. I retreated up the slope toward the town, wondering if some kind of freak storm was blowing in.

As if to confirm my thoughts, the wind picked up, became strong enough to bang loose shutters and pick up stray debris from the ground. I lifted a hand to shield my eyes as I climbed above the high tide mark, then turned to face out to sea.

Something was moving on the beach.

At first I thought it was a stray animal, a dog or cat foraging for stranded shellfish. But the movement became more general and I realized that there would have to be an entire pack of dogs to generate so much activity. Abruptly the moon peered from behind a cloud and wan light washed the beach.

I saw it clearly. Or perhaps them. I was never really sure which.

At first I thought it was some kind of giant squid, extending its tentacles along the shoreline. But then I noticed that those strange, probing limbs were articulated, straight sections a meter or so long, with a hinged joint in between. Too many hinged joints. They already extended all the way to dry land, and more of their length continued to emerge, jointed section after jointed section. They reached the top of the embankment and beyond, and I began to retreat toward the town, realizing that they were advancing as quickly as a man would normally walk. I picked up my pace to remain ahead of them.

As if sensing my presence, the skeletal limbs began to advance more quickly as well. One of them actually passed to my right, disappearing behind the furthest block of buildings. I could see at least six other limbs as well, and the surf sounds grew even more violent, as though the waves were being chopped apart by a host of intruders.

I crossed the frontage road and stopped to catch my breath. On the opposite side of the street, a mailbox fell over onto its side with a crash and I saw something moving behind it and past it, stretching ever deeper into Crayport. Glass broke somewhere behind me and I realized that I was being outflanked on either side. Panic paralyzed me for a few seconds, long enough for two more of the skeletal limbs to appear, one waving in the darkness above my head, the other slithering over the cracked pavement.

I turned and ran, covered a full block before my foot hit a patch of not quite dry seaweed and twisted beneath me. I landed hard, knocked the wind from my lungs, and ended up lying on my side. A light went on in a second story window across the street and I saw the silhouette of someone looking out through the galss. I wanted to cry out for help but there was no air in my lungs. Then, to my utter horror, I saw a shadowy movement as something dropped down past the roof of that house. There was a sharp cry, undoubtedly human, as the window literally exploded.

It pulled a young woman right out through the window. She screamed just once before she hit the ground. I hope to God she died then, but I'll never know for sure. What I do know is that her limp body was dragged back past the frontage road, and within seconds the stench was subsiding, the wind had died down, and the slithery movements all around me had stopped.

No one came out to investigate. No one else even turned on a light.

There's no adequate apology I can offer for what happened next. I don't believe that anything I could have done would have made a great difference, but that still doesn't excuse what I did. I stumbled back to Trumbull House in a state of shock, climbed into the Ford, and drove out of Crayport. I never spoke to Joan again, never even wrote her a letter. In fact, I drove to Ohio and found myself a job, vowing never to return to New England.

That might have been the end of it for me if I hadn't turned to the obituaries in the *New York Times* the other day. I am fifty-five years old now, just lost my thirtieth job. I live in a rented room and drive a car twelve years old. I have never married, never had a stable relationship after Joan.

The obituary was for Joan Trumbull, author of *Managansett Nights*, which I'd read, and *Night Duty*, which I'd never heard of. She had died in a boating accident, drowned, and was buried in Crayport Cemetery. Survived by her son, Ethan. No mention of a husband. I was kind of happy to hear she'd finally met someone else, husband or boyfriend. She deserved better than me.

Two weeks ago an old friend offered me a temporary job in Boston and I decided to break my resolution about New England. I packed everything I owned into the trunk of my Honda and headed east. It was out of my way, but I figured I owed it to Joan to at least visit her grave one time.

I have not once, in all those years, doubted what I'd seen in Crayport. There was no possible way I was ever going to spend a moment in that town after dark. I timed things so that I reached Crayport just after sunrise, and wasn't particularly surprised to discover it looked exactly the same as it had during my first visit.

I took the frontage road south to Trumbull House, let the car idle out front. It looked just the same, just as lifeless. The chickens were gone, but there was a pretty extensive rabbit run in their place. There was only one boat at the pier, and it had an outboard on the back.

I turned around and headed back into town, found the cemetery without much difficulty, hidden behind the Congregational Church. It took me almost an hour to find Joan's grave, which was well tended. It was in a portion of the cemetery physically isolated from the rest. All of the headstones there bore the name Trumbull. She was buried next to her uncle.

My visit seemed pointless now and I was impatient to be gone. My stomach was rumbling but I wasn't tempted to see if Nathan's Place was still in business. Instead, I pulled over at a convenience store to pick up some doughnuts and a hot coffee.

As I paid the taciturn cashier, a young man brushed past me and left the store, carrying a basket full of junk food. He didn't even glance in the cashier's direction, and the cashier pretended not to see him. I pocketed my change quickly, realizing the truth. This must be Joan's son, the heir to the Trumbull duty, the boy who might have been mine under other circumstances.

I stepped outside hastily. He was facing away from me, preparing to cross the street.

"Excuse me," I said quickly, floundering for an excuse to talk to him. "Could you tell me the time?"

He turned and faced me and I looked into his eyes, one green, one blue, and he said, "It's too late." And then he walked away.

PARTING SHOT

My friends tell me I'm frequently oblivious to emotional nuances, but even I noticed that Wilson Berlanger wasn't exactly the most popular man in Misquonet. He wasn't shunned, exactly. Mrs. Parsons was perfectly happy to take his money when he came into her store, and Nelson's Filling Station pumped gas into that beat up Ford truck without a moment's hesitation. But there was no unnecessary conversation, no friendly greeting, no wave of farewell.

I'd been living in Misquonet about three months the day I saw Stan Zimmer make an obscene gesture as Berlanger drove past.

"What's his problem?" I was having coffee with Jessie Bieler, toward whom I'd been feeling increasingly affectionate. We were sitting at one of the outside tables at Hibbert's Coffee Shop.

"What do you mean?" One of the things that had attracted me to Jessie was her direct manner. When we argued a point, she was logical and tenacious and never appeared evasive or uneasy. Not until that day, anyway.

"Come on, Jessie. What gives with Berlanger? You're the third person I've asked. Whenever his name comes up, people suddenly change the subject or pretend they don't know the man."

She shrugged and looked away. "People just don't like talking about him. He's an...unpleasant person."

"Unpleasant how?" I waited, but she didn't answer. "Do I need to learn the secret Misquonet handshake or something before you'll tell me?"

Jessie sighed and squirmed in her seat. "Sorry, Dan. I don't mean to be mysterious. I guess maybe we're a little bit ashamed. About the way we treat him, I mean."

I waited, but she seemed disinclined to continue until I prompted her. "So why do you?" She blinked. "Treat him that way, I mean. Does he beat his wife, vote the wrong party, or what?"

She sat back in her chair, arms folded, and looked across the street, her lips pressed together. I waited patiently until she was ready to talk.

"The Berlangers have always been strange. Old Tom Berlanger was a mean bastard with a lot of money. He fought the town council every time they did something to improve things around here. There was supposed to be a local exit from the Interstate, but Berlanger tied things up in the courts so long they moved it to Lanville instead. When I was in high school, a development company wanted to put up an office park just east of town, but Berlanger bought enough land to make it impossible. He fought the sewer system for two years, and got an injunction when the council tried to change the zoning laws. When he died, oh, about ten years back, people threw parties all over."

"And the sins of the father are visited on the son?"

"Not exactly." For a second I saw a hint of evasion in Jessie's eyes. "Wilson Berlanger is pretty strange in his own right. He never went to school with the rest of us. His parents educated him at home, or so they claimed. Rose Berlanger was just as contrary as her husband. She attended every school board meeting even though Wilson wasn't enrolled, constantly complained about the curriculum or the choice of books in the library, or the personal lives of the teachers."

"Is she still alive?"

Jessie shook her head. "Died about a year after her husband. No one knows exactly when, because Berlanger buried her himself and didn't bother to mention it to anyone until a couple of months later."

"Isn't that against the law?"

"Apparently not, if you've got enough money."

She had stalled again, so I nudged her. "Why such animosity if both troublemakers are gone. As far as I can tell, their son barely interacts with the town."

"Not directly. But people are convinced that it's bad luck to deal with the Berlangers. Ed and Virginia Grant built a house out near their property a few years back, and they were both killed in a fire two months later. The Carnells live close on the other side, and they lost all three of their kids in less than a year; a swimming accident took the eight year old, the six year old fell down the basement steps, and the five year old swallowed a bottle of his mother's anti-depressants."

"That doesn't make it Berlanger's fault."

"No, it doesn't. But the Grants' oldest boy rebuilt the house and was diagnosed with leukemia the week he finished it. Died a few months later. Lois Carnell hanged herself. Her husband insisted that

Wilson sneaked onto their property at night and sent bad thoughts into his wife's head. He took a shotgun up to the Berlanger house and shot out all the windows before they arrested him. He's been in the state hospital ever since. Even if Berlanger wasn't responsible, it seemed like bad luck to be anywhere near him."

"Unfortunate, but it doesn't sound bad enough to turn the man into a pariah."

"There's more. Warren Cooke used to raise a few chickens up that way, but he came out one morning and found them all dead. Others tried to keep stock of one kind or another, but it never worked out. And no one can keep a dog up that way. They howl all the time if they're confined, and if you let them run free, they take off and never come back. And then some kids went missing..." Her voice trailed off.

My coffee was gone. I signaled the waitress for a refill.

"Ariel Richards was the first. Fourteen years old. She went blueberrying up near Berlanger's house one Saturday. No one ever saw her again. Nicky Cross was next, twelve years old. Went off to school one morning but never got there. He used to ride his bike down Crowell Road rather than take the bus. They found the bike in an overgrown field, but no sign of the boy. Then Linda Zimmer disappeared from her own yard. Stan noticed Berlanger's truck driving by just before he realized she was gone. Linda was nine years old."

"When did all this happen?"

"Ariel was two years back, Linda six months ago."

"I assume the police cleared Berlanger."

She sighed. "They didn't find anything, if that's what you mean. They practically tore his house apart after Linda. Stan punched him and spent a couple of nights locked up. Berlanger wouldn't press charges."

"And that's it?"

"I suppose it sounds pretty circumstancial, but the truth is that bad things happen around the Berlangers, whether they're responsible or not. They happen a lot. At best, they're bad luck, at worst..." She shook her head. "I don't want to think about it. Can we talk about something else please?"

A week passed before I thought about Berlanger again. The

novel was going well; I was a full month ahead of schedule. But I hadn't quite worked out how my hero was going to escape Richard Scorpius' undersea fortress and after two days of false starts, I decided to take a one day vacation and get out of the house.

Jessie was working on the accession list at the town library and couldn't take the day off, so I resigned myself to solitary hiking in the hills outside of town. Misquonet is a beautiful place, an island of old style New England life tucked into a forgotten corner of the state. I packed myself a light lunch and started walking without any particular destination in mind.

My mind drifted into neutral and when my stomach finally insisted that I stop to eat, I wasn't sure exactly where I was. I found an old stump to sit on and finished two of my three sandwiches, chased them down with a can of beer that was no longer cold but tasted good all the same. After rearranging my pack, I oriented myself by the sun and turned in a direction that I hoped would take me back toward home.

Ten minutes later, thanks to my own carelessness, I twisted my ankle and went sprawling on my face. At first I thought I could walk off the ache, but it worsened quickly and I could only move in fits and starts.

I was hoping to spot a paved road, but instead I finally noticed the straight line of a roof through the trees. The pain had spread up through my right calf to the knee, and I was trying to decide who'd be the least inconvenienced if I called for help.

When I got a clearer view of the building, it was disheartening. The windows were boarded up, the paint was peeling, the gutters were filled with layers of dead leaves and other debris, and the grounds hadn't been tended in a very long time. I hobbled around to the front of the house, which faced a narrow dirt road, and that's when I noticed the oversized mailbox mounted on a stone pillar. The faded letters were still legible: Carnell.

I was oriented now. This was Crowell Road, paved near the town center, hard packed dirt this far out. If I turned left, I had a two mile hike before the next house. To the right, I'd come to the Berlanger place much more quickly, but the road ended there, and if Berlanger wasn't home, I'd be even further from rescue.

Well, if he wasn't home, I'd sit on his porch until he arrived. I hobbled onward.

If I hadn't been so preoccupied with the pain, I might have noticed the odd change in the foliage around me earlier than I did. It was early autumn and there were only occasional hints of color in some of the trees. At least that was true elsewhere in town. There was no clear transition, but I began to notice entire branches of dead leaves, withered to an unhealthy rusty brown, or even black. Toadstools were everywhere, nacreous white and pallid yellow, with furry undersides and swollen nodules that distorted them almost past recognition. The ever present dragonflies I'd been brushing aside for most of the morning no longer troubled me, but I saw earthworms lying motionless from time to time, erupted from the earth to dry and bloat in the sunlight. Once an oversized toad hopped out of my path, and before it disappeared into the brush I saw that its legs were mismatched in size.

I wasn't paying attention to my footing. My leg buckled under me and I fell a second time, ripping my pants and banging my knee. I cursed my clumsiness and my stupidity in not anticipating an accident of this sort and bringing my cell phone.

Ten minutes later I caught sight of the Berlanger house. It was larger than I'd expected, two stories, eight windows facing front on the second floor. The house and grounds were reasonably well kept, although a fresh coat of paint would not have been unwelcome. I couldn't see Berlanger's truck, even when I reached his driveway. I would have to wait for Berlanger to return.

There were chairs on the narrow porch and I planned to sit in one with my damaged ankle propped on another, but I slipped on the steps and managed to bang the same knee again, and this time I nearly fainted from the pain. I crawled the rest of the way onto the porch and rolled carefully onto my back, breathing slowly and deeply. The porch eaves were filled with old hornet nests and spider webs. I remember watching a particularly fat sun spider moving lazily above me but then it was mysteriously gone and I realized I'd drifted off into unconsciousness for a while.

My wristwatch said that it was only about two o'clock, but the display was frozen. It had stopped.

I managed to sit up without screaming. Encouraged, I started sliding across the rough wooden floorboards toward the nearest chair, then changed direction when I noticed that I could see into the house. The front door was open; only a screen barred the way. If it wasn't locked, I might be able to get inside, telephone for help, and then make it back out before Berlanger returned. Technically, I suppose, it would constitute illegal entry, but by now I was seriously worried about what I'd done to my leg.

The screen door was not secured.

The interior was superficially well kept. The front room was orderly and apparently heavily used, but the chairs and tables had a patina of dirt, the drapes were dark and coated with dust, and the air smelled stale and unhealthy. The walls were adorned with what appeared to be hunting trophies, but when my eyes adjusted to the murky gloom, I realized that they were goat heads, each and every one. Not mountain goats or other suitable trophies either, just simple, ordinary field goats, inexpertly mounted. Crossed sabers hung over the fireplace, an antique flintlock and a crossbow stood on the mantle. It was not a welcoming room.

There was a broom in one corner that I drafted as a crutch while I explored the ground floor. The telephone was in the incredibly cluttered kitchen, an old fashioned black box with a rotary dial. I lifted the receiver thankfully and a moment later almost threw it across the room. No dial tone. Berlanger's telephone was not working, or perhaps he'd discontinued service since no one wanted to talk to him.

I sat down at the kitchen table, pushed aside a stack of moderately clean dishes, and leaned forward, cradling my head on my arms. I told myself to rest for a few minutes, then return to my original plan and wait on the porch until Berlanger returned. But instead I fell asleep.

Shadows had crept up over the windows when I raised my head, disoriented, nearly panicking when I remembered where I was and how I had come to be there. I had to get outdoors before Berlanger returned. His unsavory reputation aside, I had no intention of being arrested for trespassing.

I stood tentatively, relieved to discover that the pain had diminished somewhat, although I still winced with every step. Slowly but with growing confidence, I started back toward the front of the house.

The exterior door was closed and a deadbolt thrown. I froze in the archway, glancing around cautiously. Through the window I could see Berlanger's truck parked under a tree. It was completely silent and there were no lights on inside the house, through which darkness was spreading like an inky flood.

I considered my options. Top priority was to legitimize my position. The door was only a few steps away. I could cross the room, slip the deadbolt, exit, then knock on the door and seek the help I'd originally planned to solicit. But no, that wouldn't work. The bolt would be thrown and I'd be unable to reset it from outside.

Leave? Hobble back to town on my own? The idea wasn't appealing. In the darkness, I might well lose my footing again. And when Berlanger discovered the thrown bolt, might he not come looking for an intruder? Although I had dismissed the town's prejudice against Berlanger as petty and unjustified, the situation seemed more fraught with danger now that I was alone, injured, and trapped in Berlanger's house in the dark.

Perhaps there was another way out.

I moved silently to the hall, seeking a back exit, even an open window. Instead I found a yawning doorway that led down into the darkness. The basement. I had half turned away when I heard the sound.

A child's cry from somewhere below.

I remembered what Jessie had said and it no longer seemed quite so implausible. The skeptical part of me tried to protest that I was letting my imagination run wild, that I'd misheard a perfectly innocent sound, but before I could turn away, it came again, this time more distinctly, and I knew that I would have to go down those stairs, that I couldn't just turn and leave.

The stairway was narrow and dark, the steps rough and uneven. I was terrified of falling, or making a sound that would alert Berlanger to my presence. I extended one hand in front of me to ward off unseen obstructions and ran the other along the wall to brace myself. A sticky, syrupy coating stuck to the tips of my fingers, and the smell rising from the basement, subtle at first, grew increasingly strong, rancid, a blend of all things sour and corrupt.

There was a lightbulb mounted at the foot of the stairs, but its glow was muted. I reached the last step and paused, hoping my eyes would adjust to the dim light. The usual basement clutter was piled up on my left. To the right, a furnace and an oil tank flanked the opening of a narrow passageway. I heard a faint movement from that direction, but no repetition of the child's cry.

A length of corroded piping lay on the floor and I crouched to retrieve it. It wasn't much of a weapon, but I didn't feel quite so helpless. My heart racing, I lurched forward into the passageway. From ahead, I thought I heard someone singing, but the words were indistinct.

The passageway took a sharp right turn and I stopped, blinking as my eyes adjusted to the light. A greenish glow spread from what seemed to be a hole in the floor. Clutching the pipe so tightly that my fingers ached, I moved forward.

There was indeed a hole. A roughly circular plug of cement was canted up on oversized hinges, revealing a steep stairway that led down into yet another level. Even in that pallid light, I recognized that the lower chamber's entrance would be completely concealed if the plug were lowered. I remembered the missing children, and the fruitless search by police.

The singing was louder now. A man's voice, rough, unmelodic. Sometimes I thought I could almost understand the words. I half turned, terror demanding that I quit this place, bad leg or not, and run for help. But then a child's voice interrupted the singing, which stopped abruptly. The man spoke harshly and there was a moment of silence before he resumed.

Leaving now was out of the question. I moved to the very brink and peered over, but all I could see from that vantage point was the stairs themselves. Suddenly ashamed of my hesitation, I began to descend.

Even remembering the scene that awaited me brings out a cold sweat. The lower chamber was quite large but imperfectly lighted. At the end farthest from where I entered, Wilson Berlanger stood with his back toward me, facing what I initially thought was an enormous glass globe. To one side, a young girl perhaps twelve years old sat in an oversized wooden chair. Her wrists were secured to its arms, but she seemed otherwise unharmed, though her head was bowed and I could not see her face.

Berlanger was singing again, or chanting actually, mostly in some obscure gibberish that conveyed no meaning to me. But from time to time he would break into impassioned English, and those snatches of intelligible words chilled me to the marrow.

"Manifest yourself, my Lord! Break the barriers of time and

space to greet your servant!"

Berlanger, I assumed immediately, was some kind of satanist. But I was wrong.

I advanced cautiously, brandishing the pipe, wondering if I was justified in striking the man from behind. It seemed cowardly, somehow, but I knew that if the chance came, I would take it. Under ordinary circumstances, I was probably a physical match for the man, but I wasn't nearly as mobile as I wished to be.

Something moved within the globe. The motion caught my attention and I froze, still perhaps fifteen feet from Berlanger. My eyes strained to make out the contours of the thing, which resolved itself into the semblance of a goat's head, although there were oddities of perspective or from that made it impossible for my eyes to bring it into clear focus. Those things which might be ears seemed to twist in an impossible direction. The horns were asymmetrical and changed shape every few seconds. The jaws weren't right; they seemed hinged to open horizontally as well as vertically. And there were too many eyes.

"Goat with a Thousand Young!" Berlanger screamed at the top of his lungs. "I have brought the living key,! If this one pleases you more than the others, then reward your servant by opening the Gate so that I might feel your presence!" And then he was off on another string of gibberish.

The substance of the globe wavered and something began to emerge, something indescribable. It was as though fingers of pure energy were reaching out. They had no color, no substance, but they distorted the space through which they passed and I found it distinctly painful to look at them directly. There were at least a dozen strands of this peculiar phenomenon, and they moved directly toward the imprisoned child. I froze, stunned, but the child's eyes widened and she screamed. The tentative progress became suddenly purposeful and before I could react, the groping strands reached their victim.

It was mercifully brief. The pallid tendrils engulfed face and torso in an instant. The child struggled for only a second or two, then sank back motionless as the tenuous fingers of force enfolded her completely.

"She is stronger than the others, Great One. Grasp the key and make it your own!" Berlanger had turned to face the child, but hadn't seemed to notice me, although I was now at the edge of his line of sight. "Turn the key and open the Gate!"

The head that was not after all that of a goat seemed to swell within the globe, filled it completely, and its substance darkened and became more distinct. Things moved over its dark hide, but whether they were some obscene parasite or simply another part of its own vile substance, I could not tell.

From the child's head, new tendrils began to erupt, but these were not the tenuous strands I'd seen before. These were solid, impossibly massive, and they grew in length and girth so rapidly that they brushed the ceiling and side walls. The stench of corruption assaulted my nose with such intensity that my stomach churned.

The pipe fell from my hand and I turned and fled, ignoring the pain in my leg as utter panic superseded all other sensation. If I had not fallen over a chair in the front room and banged my injured knee, I might not have had another rational thought until I was far from Berlanger's house, lost in the darkness.

But I did fall, and the pain drove away some of the terror, enough that I began to feel ashamed of my headlong flight. The child remained below, possibly still alive although I could not imagine how. I staggered to my feet and leaned against the fireplace, fighting for calm.

My fingers brushed the flintlock. To my surprise, it was well maintained. Unfortunately, there was neither powder nor shot to accompany it. But the crossbow was in equally good condition, and one quarrel was already mounted. A second lay beside it on the mantle.

I was reaching for it when the floor erupted under me.

The tentacle, if that's the right word, burst through rotted wood and uncoiled into the front room. Its movements were themselves unnatural, more of a flow of substance than the contraction of muscles. I grabbed the crossbow and quarrel and moved quickly away, and another explosion from behind warned me that the creature was bursting through the floor in other locations as well. The carpeting in front of me convulsed and the front window exploded as a supporting beam split. Moonlight spilled into the house and I saw things more distinctly. The tentacles were studded irregularly with large nodules and the one nearest to me looked vaguely like a human face.

Access to the basement was still clear and I half walked, half ran in that direction, ignoring the pain in my leg. The house shuddered when I was halfway down and I almost lost my footing, but at last I reached the bottom and turned toward the horrid altar I'd seen before.

That end of the chamber boiled with motion. Tentacles slithered around the outer walls, pressed against the ceiling. I saw at least four places where the creature had burst through into the house above. Berlanger stood beside the globe, his face twisted in ecstasy. The child sat beside him, rigid, her body the conduit into which flowed the immaterial substance of the beast, out of which flowed cables of revolting flesh that thickened into massive tentacles.

The light was better down here and I saw more detail; the nodules I'd noticed were in fact human faces, faces twisted into grimaces of eternal horror. One of them opened its eyes and looked at me as I walked past.

I could not hope to kill this horror with a flimsy arrow, no matter how well aimed, but Berlanger was another matter. He saw me at the last moment, his eyes narrowing with hatred, but made no move to evade my shot. The range was so short that I was certain I could fire a fatal bolt, but the ground shook beneath me and the quarrel embedded itself in his shoulder instead of his heart.

He didn't even wince.

"You cannot harm the Servant!" He crowed, glancing at the creature in the globe. "Not in the Master's presence!" And so saying, he reached up and pulled out the bolt, tossing it away with an exaggerated flourish. Blood oozed from the wound for only a few seconds.

"We have to stop this thing, Berlanger!" I struggled to mount the second quarrel. "It will destroy all of us!"

"Not all of us, you fool! Only the chattels, the low folk with the minds of slaves who believe themselves the masters. But the true Master has returned at last and I have provided the key. Those who have scorned me shall know my wrath at last."

I raised the crossbow to my shoulder and Berlanger laughed at me, laughed with such obvious confidence that I knew it would do no good. Even if he died, the cataclysm he'd initiated would continue now.

During the next pause between tremors, I adjusted my aim

and fired the bolt.

How I escaped that house I shall never know. The stairs to the ground floor collapsed under my feet and it was only through desperation that I leaped forward, scrambling up into the house proper. By then the thrashing tentacles had already brought down much of the roof, and the contents of the second floor rained on me as I staggered toward the doorway. Once I leaped over a tentacle, and then I fell against another. But already they were shrinking, losing their substance, retreating back to the hidden chamber and presumably to that other reality where such horrors exist.

I fell off the porch just as the front wall collapsed and rolled away as splinters of wood fell about me. Something struck my head and I lost consciousness for a while. I'm not sure how long, but it was full dark when I opened my eyes.

Dark and silent.

Berlanger's house was gone. Where it had stood there was an enormous pit filled with splintered wood and unidentifiable debris. The moon had risen and there was enough light to show me that no trace of the house remained.

Berlanger's keys were in his truck. I abandoned it two blocks from my house and limped the rest of the way home.

The official explanation was that a sinkhole opened up on the Berlanger property. Tentative efforts to locate Berlanger's body, but several minor accidents occurred at the excavation site and efforts were finally discontinued. Unofficially, the people of Misquonet believed the Devil took Berlanger to Hell. The truth, if it were known, is probably far worse.

The disappearance that same day of twelve year old Mandy Miller remains unsolved, as does that of Ariel Richards, Nikky Cross, and Linda Zimmer. No one even speculates about their fate, and only I know what shape it must have taken. Berlanger's first three victims were, presumably, failed attempts. Either they died during the ceremony, or Berlanger disposed of them after they proved themselves inadequate vessels. I wonder if their faces were among those embedded on that vile creature's skin. The three earlier children must, I feel certain, have died horribly.

But Mandy Miller's was a cleaner death. The quarrel hit her directly between the eyes, exactly where I'd aimed it. The circuit, or whatever it was, was severed when she died and the gate was locked again.

I hope that the details of that ceremony died with Berlanger, but whenever I hear that a child has disappeared, no matter where it happened, I have difficulty sleeping and wake with phantom pain in my now healed leg and my heart beating wildly in my chest.

BAD SOIL

The effect was first noticeable in the high school tennis court but within days it had replicated itself in one fashion or another all through the area.

I had the luck, if that's the appropriate term, to be present at the very first. Not that I play tennis myself. I've neither the reach nor the stamina to excel, and I've never been happy committing myself to any activity I could not perform well. But at fourteen my niece Rianne was firmly committed to the sport and I occasionally consented to be her escort to the courts. The handful of young boys who regularly convened in the area had never offered her any harm, but they were rowdy and disrespectful and I know Rianne and her friend Julie felt better for my presence.

They'd been volleying for an hour or so and I was getting restless. I had vowed to finish the ninth chapter of my book by the weekend and I was already two full days behind my self imposed schedule.

Just as I was about to suggest that we leave, Julie managed a quite nice backhand that almost caught Rianne flatfooted. She recovered quickly, driving across the court and toward the net. The ball dropped to the ground at a sharp angle, but Rianne was already anticipating its trajectory. Her arm cut the air gracefully as she extended her body in a perfect maneuver.

But her racket swished through empty air, for the ball had stopped dead the moment it struck the ground. In one of her less graceful moments, Rianne staggered and fell to one knee.

This seemed a perfect moment to call it a day, so I arose and approached. Julie seemed to sense the same thing, and had already come cross court. But Rianne remained where she was, staring at the motionless ball a few feet away.

"What happened?" I asked unnecessarily. "Bad ball?"

Julie scooped it up, tossed it lightly into the air and caught it on her racket. "Feels okay to me. Must've been a soft spot in the ground."

Rianne stood up awkwardly and I could see she'd skinned her knee. "I never had that happen before. Let me see."

Julie tossed her the ball. Rianne bounced it off the ground, caught it, bounced it again. Thoughtfully she walked past her friend toward the net, paused, bounced it a third time.

The ball hit the ground and remained there.

I joined her as she knelt, running her fingers across the clay. "There must be a bad spot," I suggested.

Rianne looked puzzled. "We play here all the time. I've never noticed this before."

But we could feel the difference. Although the surface looked the same, it felt soft, moist, vaguely repulsive. It was exactly the sensation one gets picking up a piece of bad fruit.

Mrs. Parkhurst's garden went bad that same day. I heard her complaining in Del's Hardware when I stopped by for lightbulbs just before supper.

"There must've been something bad in that fertilizer you sold me, Delbert Scott. Everything was fine until I used it. Now all the plants are dying."

"It's not the fertilizer, Minnie. I told you, I use it all the time at home."

"Well you just come over then and tell me what's wrong with my flowers. This morning they were all bright and healthy, and this afternoon they're flat on the ground. My prize roses are already mush."

"If it's not insects, it must be something in the soil. You're downhill from the printshop, aren't you? Maybe they dumped something into the ground and it's washed down to your property."

They were still arguing when I paid for my purchases and left.

The Crawley Street bridge collapsed some time during the night. Eve Goddard discovered it on her way to work. Unfortunately, she discovered it my driving off the edge. Fortunately, her little Fiat bottomed out and got hung up on the edge rather than falling into Murly Chasm.

"Damnedest thing I've ever seen." Marty Carlisle was milking the incident for all it was worth, talking so loud at Kat's Kafe that we could hear him all the way over on the opposite side of the diner. "The bridge supports all look fine. But the ground went soft under the north abutment and the bridge just let go. Soil's so bad, you stab a knife into it, the blade just falls right over. Nothing there to hold it up. But it's not like beach sand either. It's more like wood punk. You know, no body to it."

I was thinking about the tennis court but just about then Kat put a bowl of stew in front of me and I never made the connection. Not till later.

Not till Rianne came to see me.

It was three days after the bridge incident and I was finally back on schedule with my book. Months of research at the Arkham and Sheffield Libraries had convinced me that there was a link between the strange madness that had infected the town of Dunwich and the so-called "quiet riot" in Managansett in the late 19th Century, and I had enough material to produce a book on the subject, if I could just enforce the self discipline necessary to bring it to fruition.

The front door opened. "Hello, Rianne." I never kept it locked, but I knew she was the only one who would enter without knocking first.

"Hi, Uncle Bob. Can I come in?"

"A little late to be asking, isn't it?" The exchange was our regular greeting. "What's up?"

Rianne settled into the sofa and curled up with her legs underneath. She was a pretty child, spoiled rotten by her parents, not so much innocent as oblivious. Frankly, I thought her parents sheltered her a bit too much. At times, she acted well below her age, petulant, self centered, prone to fits of giggling that were decidedly unattractive. But in her better moments she could be charming, honestly affectionate, and clever. She often made me regret that Elaine and I had deferred a family until too late, and then the cancer made it all impossible.

"Do you remember that day on the tennis court?"

I raised my eyebrows. "Which day was that, might I ask? We were last there Tuesday, but also Saturday, Friday, and the previous Wednesday. I remember distinctly because I've been up past midnight these past three days trying to make up all the time I've lost escorting you here and there."

"It was only a few hours, Uncle Bob, and you told me there's no real deadline for your book anyway."

"Just my own," I admitted. "But standards are important, Rianne, even if they're artificial ones."

"Yes, sir," she answered with mock gravity.

"So what brings you here today?" I glanced out the window. A steady drizzle had started during the night and showed no sign of abating. "Not tennis, obviously."

"Not exactly. You remember when Julie made that shot and we found the bad spot in the clay?"

"Yes, of course I do. How's the knee, incidentally?"

"Fine," she said dismissively. "The thing of it is, I found a couple of other places like that out near our house. Places where the grass died and the dirt is mushy."

Rianne's family lived a block from Mrs. Parkhurst, I recalled. "I wonder if there's something seeping into the soil. One of your neighbors mentioned the same thing the other day." I massaged my chin. "What does your father say?"

"Oh, you know Dad. He shrugs his shoulders and says tiny flying saucers must've landed during the night."

"Well, I'm sure it's nothing to worry about." But for the first time, I wasn't so sure.

"Yeah, well, the thing is, I asked a few of my friends and some of them noticed the same kinds of things. Like, Mr. Pratt stepped into a pothole in his own backyard and broke an ankle. And Kelly Witherspoon's collie died in his doghouse two nights ago and when they tried to move him, his body was all stuck to the ground and they had to use a shovel. And that big elm tree next to the Donovan's patio lost all its leaves and a couple of days later the trunk just split in two and half of it fell on the roof of their garage."

I raised my hands to stop the tide of words. "What do these things have to do with one another, Rianne? Trees die, so do dogs. And people have accidents."

She sighed theatrically and glanced up at the ceiling. "I'm trying to tell you, Uncle Bob, that there's something wrong in the ground around here lately. There's lots more things I haven't told you yet, like Mr. Whalen's swimming pool collapsing and the sewer lines backing up into the school basement and stuff like that."

I wasn't convinced but I was disquieted. "Rianne, this sounds like a lot of coincidences to me, but I'll tell you what. I'll ask around and see what I can find out."

"Great. And I'll keep gathering evidence." She held up a small notebook I hadn't noticed. "I've been writing everything down and Daddy said he'd bring me home a town map from the office so I could plot them all. I know something's going on, Uncle Bob. I just know it."

I did make a few inquiries. Chief Connors and I went to school together and we still played cards occasionally.

"There have been a few complaints," he admitted. "Andrews called down to the university and they had some people come up and take samples. They couldn't find anything wrong, just poor soil, they said. The Printworks people deny they've been dumping anything and Matt Carson's a pretty square guy. Could be they had a leak they don't know about, but Bud Nelson found a bad spot in his hay field and that's uphill and way the other side of town."

Dr. Gates, the veterinarian, admitted the state of the dog's body was unusual. "If you ask me, he'd been dead a couple of days not just a few hours. Too much decomposition even if it was a warm night."

Andrews, the Town Engineer, was openly skeptical. "People are too quick to blame pollution for everything that goes wrong. I had some samples taken to calm things down, but if you ask me, there's nothing to it. But you know how these things take on a life of their own, Bob. One person remarks on a coincidence, and everyone else starts making connections in their minds and the whole thing grows on itself until you have a panic."

Two days later, little Mickey Walker wandered away from his yard when his mother went in to answer the phone and forgot to watch him. He was only four years old and the woodlot was less than a hundred acres, but the search parties found no trace of him at all. What they did find was a churned up piece of ground about ten feet in diameter where all the grass had rotted to dust and the surrounding brush had died back.

Carl Cellucci told me about it that same evening. "Looked like someone set a fire there, except there wasn't any ash or anything. But the ground sure looked burnt all to hell, and it felt funny walking on it. Spongy like."

Kidnappers were suspected, but there was nothing to hint at

their identity. No strange cars or people in the neighborhood.
Rianne called to tell me that half a dozen pets had disappeared
during the week, and that she was plotting everything on the map her
father had brought home.

"I've got it on the wall in my bedroom and there's red
pushpins where things've happened."

"Sounds helpful," I said calmly. The truth was that I was
getting concerned. Independent of the possible existence of a real
danger in the soil was the threat of mass hysteria. Dunwich and
Managansett had erupted into violence when strings of apparent
coincidences were woven into a consistent though irrational pattern.
I would hate to see the same phenomenon repeated at first hand.

I woke up the following morning to find myself without
power or telephone. Unshaven, unshowered, and uncoffee'd, I drove
toward town to file a complaint, but ran into the workcrew two
blocks from my house.

"Morning, Mr. Crane." Harry Feldon waved at me. "Had a
little problem here this morning." He gestured toward the utility
pole, which lay crumpled across the road. "We'll have this out of the
way in a couple of minutes. It'll be a while yet before we can get a
new pole in though."

"What happened?" I had pulled over and leaned out through
the car window.

"Damned if I know. The pole just went right over. Bottom's
all rotted out, looks like. Don't you worry though. We'll get it all
fixed up before you know it."

But it was noon before the power was back on. They had to
sink the new pole four times before they found a spot where the soil
would support its weight.

I drove over to my brother's to use their shower and sink.
Rianne was out already and her mother seemed concerned.

"I don't know what's gotten into that girl lately. She hasn't
played tennis in days, she's on the phone constantly, and when she's
not on the phone she's acting mysterious and writing things in her
new diary."

"School starts back up in another couple of weeks, Erin.
She's just trying to cram a whole summer into the last few days.
She'll be fine."

I hoped.

Uncharacteristically, I never even entered my office during that day. The power loss had thrown my schedule sufficiently off that I devoted the afternoon to grocery shopping, dropping off my shirts to be laundered, and running various other errands. I ate out and stopped by Twin Elms Tavern for a drink that expanded to three when Del Scott walked in. I was in bed half an hour after arriving home.

The phone wakened me just before eleven. It was Erin.

"You haven't heard from Rianne today, have you, Bob?"

"No, she hasn't been by. Is something wrong?"

"Well, she's past her curfew. I called Tim and Julie and some of the rest of the kids but none of the ones I reached know anything."

"Did she say where she was going?" I asked inanely.

"No, she rushed out this morning and came back sometime during the afternoon while I was shopping. She was already gone again when I came home."

"Probably just lost track of time." I struggled to keep the concern out of my voice.

"I suppose so. But she's been so preoccupied lately. Sorry to have bothered you, Bob."

"Nonsense. And give me a call when she comes in, will you? Just so I won't worry either."

Unable to sleep, I brewed some tea and wandered into my study, and the brink of nightmare. Rianne had left a note on my desk, anchored by my gargoyle paperweight.

"Dear Uncle Bob," I read. "I think I found something. The bad soil all points to one place. We're going to check it out. We waited for you but it's going to get dark soon so we have to hurry. Love you. Rianne."

Ten minutes later I was dressed and driving.

"Bob?" Erin's face dropped when I got out of the car. Obviously she'd been hoping to see someone else.

"Where's Frank?"

"He's out," she answered vaguely. "Trying to find her. Tim Krenkle is missing too." Tim was Rianne's current boyfriend.

"I need to look at something in her room." I brushed past without waiting for an answer.

The map was bigger than I had expected, a large plat map from her father's realty office. As she had described, there were pushpins marking all of the "incidents" she knew of.

The pattern was obvious.

All of the pins could be grouped into straight lines, each radiating from a common center. Judging by the scale, they extended as much as five miles from the source, reaching almost to the town limits in every direction.

"What is it, Bob?"

"I don't know. I'll be back in a while, Erin. I need to check on something."

And then I was driving toward the dam.

I parked on the road just downstream from Stauley Dam and climbed the fence designed to keep people from falling into Murly Chasm. The incline was steep, but I'd climbed it scores of times as a boy. It was a bit difficult now that I was in my forties, and the darkness didn't help any, but I managed to reach the bottom with nothing worse than a bruised hip.

The dam towered over me. The sluice gates were closed on this side; they hadn't been opened in four years that I knew of. Murly Chasm was the emergency outflow to bleed off excess water, and we'd had a non-critical shortage for that period. A lot had happened in that time. I resigned as town engineer after Elaine died, made my living as a freelance writer and occasional consultant to the town council. No one knew the dam and the immediate area as well as I did; I'd been project engineer when it was constructed twenty years earlier.

So I knew right away that something was wrong.

This part of the chasm should have been a gently rolling flatland overshadowed by the steep walls to either side. The walls will still there, but the ground had changed shape. Instead of a concave swelling, it was convex, a depression leading off into a declivity I'd never seen before. I stepped forward and the ground felt unnaturally soft under my feet. My feet seemed to sink into the soil as though it were made of pudding.

There was a cave in the side of the hill to my right, a cave that had never been there before. I flicked on my flashlight and descended into darkness.

For the most part, the passage was high enough to walk normally, although occasionally I was forced to duck under obstructions. I found their footprints right away, although the soil was already dissolving and flowing in to fill the depressions. Rianne obviously wasn't alone because I read two different brand names in the patterns.

I thought to call out her name, but refrained, perhaps warned by some instinctive sense of self preservation.

The decline steepened as I continued.

I found Tim Krenkle ten minutes later. By that time I had descended an unknown but not inconsiderable distance into the Earth, and I had lost the last vestiges of my former skepticism. This was no natural phenomenon, I knew. The tunnels were purposive, artificially straight. I paused once to examine the walls and found thick striations of dessicated soil, veins of earth that had been somehow transformed, lessened, robbed of some vitality of content that left them spongy, crumbling, and subtly foul.

Tim was lying at the first intersection of the tunnel I followed with a second, and I literally stumbled over his remains. And "remains" is the operative word here, because part of Tim Krenkle was undeniably missing. His flesh had fallen in over his bones, his face was a terrifying parody of a humanity, lips drawn back from the teeth, eyes sunken. I crouched and touched his chest and the ribcage gave way even though my touch was tentative, an indentation that remained when I removed my hand.

Footprints led off to the right.

I was remembering some of the claims made by survivors of the "quiet riot" in Managansett, the insane insistence that a creature or creatures had emerged from beneath the Earth to claim victim after victim, a charge that could not be supported by fact. Thirty eight people died in Managansett that night, and another dozen disappeared, but there was no evidence that their deaths could have been attributed to anything other than the mass insanity of their neighbors.

But I remembered references to a Cthonian race and their dread god Shudde-M'ell and I felt the sweat breaking out all over my body. My steps faltered and I hesitated, telling myself that I was better off summoning help than proceeding unaided. There could be vast caverns down here, and I could not hope to search them myself.

Almost I turned and retraced my steps, but at that very moment I heard a sound, something between a sob and a sigh, and I shrugged off my shameful fears and plunged forward.

The footprints led me through two more intersections. At each, the trail grew momentarily confused, as though Rianne had hesitated, trying to decide how to proceed. But in each case, she had continued straight ahead.

There were other tracks as well, though I didn't recognize them at first. There were lines in the soil, as though metallic cables had been dragged across the ground. At first I dismissed them as a natural formation, but at each divergent path, they unerring turned to follow the Nike prints.

And I followed them both.

And emerged into an enormous chamber. I am tempted to call it an amphitheatre, because that's what it most closely resembled. I was standing in a kind of balcony level, a narrow ledge that skirted the main chamber. There was a second balcony below me, halfway to the floor, and crumbling slopes analogous to staircases connected each to one another and the floor.

Two levels below me, a diminutive human body lay in a tangle. From this distance, my flash couldn't illuminate enough for me to make out the details, but the body was prone, covered by a mesh of ropes or tendrils or something similar. Every few seconds the body would heave and an arm or leg would thrash about briefly, then subside.

I almost fell as I ran down to the main gallery.

From near at hand, I felt my gorge rise. What I had taken to be ropes were revealed to be much more animate, pale elongated worms whose outer integument was covered with wiry filaments. Their victim was so completely covered that I could no longer see her features, and it was clear that the fibers had penetrated her flesh. They throbbed with obscene life as they drew from her body the same essence they apparently extracted from the very soil around them.

"Rianne! My God!" My whisper was hoarse, horrified.

"Uncle Bob!" The voice was unexpectedly vibrant, and it came from behind me. I whirled and saw her emerge from a side passage.

"Rianne?" I took a hesitant step in her direction.

"Run! Oh, please run, Uncle Bob!"

Even as she spoke, the body beside me gave one final heave, then subsided, sinking into itself, into the soil beneath it. And those horrid, wormlike tendrils withdrew and began questing for fresh sustenance, cilia testing the air as if to smell out their prey. I swept the area with my flashlight and discovered to my horror that neither were they discrete individuals, but rather that their individual threads all led into a single side tunnel, in the depths of which I caught only a passing glimpse of unimaginable horror.

Something lurked there, some central body from which these wormlike things emerged, something so obscenely unnatural that it's very appearance was an affront to nature. There were angles to the thing that seemed to twist in impossible directions, into other dimensions.

I ran to Rianne's side, barely able to control my rising gorge.

"Who?" I whispered, nodding back at the now motionless corpse.

"Julie," she answered tearfully, catching hold of my arm. "Uncle Bob, I'm so scared."

"Let's get out of here." I nodded back toward the way I'd come."

"They won't let us leave." She was shaking her head distractedly.

"Nonsense." Had I been on my own, I might have descended into gibbering panic. But I had Rianne to worry about, and I refused to let her down. "Let's go."

I led her back up to the first balcony level. Below us, the fibrous tendrils had spread across the gallery floor, a carpet of giant maggots questing for warm flesh.

We had nearly reached the top level when I sensed rather than heard something above us. Rianne's fingers tightened painfully, pressing into my arm, and I paused, raising the flashlight.

Something moved above us, waiting at the topmost level. I didn't see it clearly, but it recoiled from the beam of my light, retreating into the passageway behind it.

"They're afraid of the light, but I lost mine when they caught Julie." Rianne's voice sounded unnaturally calm.

"Well, we won't lose mine then, will we?" And I advanced toward that unseen horror, leading Rianne away from the pit.

I don't remember everything about our retreat from that pit of Hell. Every time we passed a side tunnel we heard movement, but I flicked my light toward those sounds and they quickly retreated. All but the worms.

They nearly caught us at the last intersection, emerging from the right and pouring over the side walls. I saw the soil shrink away where they landed, but only briefly. With Rianne's wrist in one hand and the flashlight in the other, I broke into a run, never stopping, never looking back until we reached the mouth of the cave.

There was a rushing sound behind and below us, almost like water pouring through a tube, but I knew that it was something very unlike water.

Rianne started toward the chasm side but I held her wrist, pulled her in the opposite direction.

"There's a ladder up ahead," I explained. "We'll climb the dam."

At that moment, I was thinking only of rapid escape, but on our torturous climb up the concrete face of the dam, another thought occurred to me. By the time we reached the top, I had made a decision.

"This way."

I led Rianne to the main control room. The door was locked, but I had never returned my key when I resigned and I used it now to open the door. We secured it behind us, and Rianne collapsed into a chair as I approached the sluice gate controls.

It had been a while, but there'd been no reason to change anything. It took no more than five minutes to override the safety interlocks, and then I pressed down hard on the Execute button.

The sluice gates opened wide, and water began flowing into Murly Chasm. And into the cavern from which we'd escaped. We didn't leave until the chasm had turned into a small lake, from which bubbles of unclean air emerged periodically with bloated, popping sounds.

Officially, I was charged with vandalism, though I have enough friends in town that there were never any legal repercussions. Rianne is now attending private school in Providence and aside from a severe claustrophobia that doesn't seem to respond to therapy, she seems unaffected by her experiences. Indeed, she never alludes to them and her mind may have protectively shielded those memories away.

The disappearance of Julie Evans and Tim Krenkle has never been explained.

There were no more odd problems with the earth in our town after that evening, though none of the dead spots have yet regained their ordinary vigor. There have been rumors of strange soil deficiencies from a remote area of New Hampshire, but I have not investigated and do not plan to do so.

And my book? Well, it hasn't proceeded a single word beyond where it was that night. Because my thesis was that mass hysteria had been responsible for the panics that tormented these two disparate communities, panics with no basis in reality.

And now I'm not so sure.

THE THING IN THE LIBRARY

Brandon Yates was not a man with many friends. In fact he had no friends at all, really, a charge that he would have denied heatedly if it had been uttered in his presence. His chosen profession was not the sort that provided many opportunities for social interaction, and in fact he greatly preferred being allowed to work alone, choosing his own hours, undistracted by small talk or the necessity to interact with others whose priorities differed from his own. The need to travel regularly did not contribute to his social life.

Yates made his living by cataloguing the possessions of other people – specifically, books, manuscripts, correspondence, and other documents. He was happiest when surrounded by chaotic collections of such material out of which he would create order, and a comprehensive index, suitably annotated. This does not mean that Yates was a man forever trapped in another age. He made use of modern tools – computers and databases and scanners and more. There was no incongruity in his situation, despite appearances.

Most of his income came from libraries and universities which either desired to update their own recordkeeping or had been recently presented with substantial gifts which they lacked the resources to properly evaluate on their own. Occasionally he accepted work from private individuals – usually for insurance purposes or as part of the evaluation of a legacy – but only when he needed the money badly. Families and such were more likely to want to chat, to keep him company, to express their own uneducated opinions, and to otherwise interfere with the smooth flow of work which he cultivated. But every once in a while he was approached about a collection that caught his interest, such as was the case with the Winslow estate.

It was not his first visit to Newport, although it was the first time he had been there on business. One summer he had devoted the better part of three weeks to touring the mansions that were open to the public, not just the famous ones like the Breakers that had regular hours but those you could visit by appointment only. The Winslow mansion had not been one of those and in fact he hadn't heard of it until recently. Old Man Winslow was still alive back then, estranged from his family and perforce living alone among the forty-eight rooms. His cook and the cleaning people resided elsewhere and he had long since dispensed with his butler. Otis Winslow had survived into his nineties, outliving both of his sons and one of his two grandchildren, neither of whom he had ever met. It was the sole survivor of the family line who had hired Yates.

"It's all a jumble and frankly not very clean. I had a crew go over the library, kitchen, and two of the bedrooms, but most of the rest hasn't been touched. The materials in question are mostly in the library anyway." Arthur Winslow had apparently visited the mansion once following his grandfather's death, arranged for security and necessary maintenance until the property could be sold. "It doesn't meet code. That alone will eat a half million of the estate. And it may be six months before I can start drawing on the funds. He died intestate. Very inconsiderate."

Given the description and some photographs that he had been provided, Yates had estimated that it would take thirty days just to do a preliminary sort and survey. "And I can't promise that anything will be of particular value, you understand."

Winslow patently did not understand, but he accepted the situation. "I've arranged for you to stay in the mansion as you requested. The cook has been discharged, I'm afraid, but you're welcome to use the kitchen. The caretaker won't be much help; he'd never been on the property until I hired him a month back and he only stops in from time to time to make sure nothing is wrong."

Yates had indicated that he thought he could manage.

His flight was delayed so he arrived too late in the evening to hunt up the caretaker. He stayed at a hotel and kept the receipt for his expense charges. In the morning he took a cab to Bournemouth Temporary Services and only had to wait a short while for the taciturn but not unfriendly Abraham Cabot to show up. Cabot was an older man, grizzled and with a full beard and a Yankee accent so strong that Yates thought he was being made fun of. "We expected you yesterday, Mr. Yates."

"My plane got in late. Sorry, but I didn't have a number to call to let you know."

"No matter. I'm due for a walk through today anyway. My car is out front." The trip only took a few minutes, during which Yates was told that Cabot visited the mansion three times weekly to check for rodents, vandals, plumbing problems, etc. The cleaning people came in on Wednesdays, but they were only responsible for the rooms that had already been rehabilitated. "I come by and let them in. They don't have their own key."

The mansion was well away from the tourist areas, near Brenton Cove although not on the water. It was completely surrounded by trees and the narrow driveway was so overgrown that Yates didn't notice it until Cabot abruptly turned the wheel. The grounds were unkempt but not entirely overgrown except behind the house itself, which Yates thought looked rather institutional. It was rectangular and bore no ornamentation other than the pillared entranceway. Ivy and other growth covered most of the walls, even in front.

"The roof's sound so you won't have to worry about the rain getting in, but it's a bit drafty and the nights are getting cooler. The chimneys need work before the fireplaces can be used and the heating system isn't all that efficient so I've had an electric space heater put in your room in case you need it."

"Thank you, but I'm quite used to the cold." He had spent the previous winter working for a private library in Bangor. September in Newport seemed almost tropical.

Cabot parked in front of the front door. He took one of Yates' bags, for which he was immensely grateful. The lock was massive and the key proportional. It was obviously old but it moved smoothly and the heavy door was so well balanced that Cabot opened it without effort.

They stepped into an impressive but not overly impressive hall. A wide stairway stood directly in front of them, splitting into two wings as it ascended. There were windows at the distant rear but they were curtained and allowed little light into the room. Cabot touched the light switch and four strategically placed lamps lit up the space – inadequately.

"Winslow wasn't much of one for bright lighting. He wired up the library real proper and the kitchen is okay, but he never got around to the rest of the house. " Cabot gestured to a line of sconces along one wall, the nearest of which still showed the stub of a candle. There was a matching line on the other side. "I had the circuit to the library checked because Mr. Winslow, that's Arthur

Winslow, told us you would need to use a computer. The electrician said it was enough to run a small factory."

"Yes, I have my laptop with me. Two of them in fact."

"Shouldn't be a problem, but I wouldn't try plugging them in elsewhere."

The tour was rather perfunctory. The library was immense, out of all proportion to the rest of the house, and filled with a labyrinthine pattern of shelving and internal walls. "The light in here isn't great. I guess he never got around to having more fixtures installed. There's a work light with a long extension cord in one of the desk drawers."

A plaque was hung over the entranceway bearing the date December 16, 1987. "What's the significance of the date?" Cabot had no idea.

The kitchen was definitely from another age. "No microwave, and I wouldn't try running one in here anyway. I suppose you could use it in the library. Icebox works fine even though it looks pretty clunky. The water is drinkable but sometimes it comes out dark because of rust in the pipes. Let it run for a while and it clears up. Or at least it has so far."

There was a functioning bathroom downstairs. The dining room was surprisingly small, as was another room that seemed to have no purpose. "I don't suppose old Winslow did much entertaining, but when he did, it was probably in here. Hasn't been cleaned yet so I'd give it a wide berth."

Upstairs, two bedrooms had been made presentable, across the main hall from one another. Cabot steered him in the one to the right. "There's nothing to distinguish one from the other, except that I've put whatever I thought you might need in this one."

The lights were slightly brighter than downstairs, but not significantly so.

"Was this Winslow's own bedroom?" asked Yates.

Cabot shook his head. "We didn't want to put you in there, sir. You know that's where the old man died?"

"No, I didn't."

"Well, frankly, it smells bad in there. We tried cleaning everything but the cleaning didn't take exactly. It was a few days before they found him and it was the middle of August last year."

"The whole place smells musty," Yates said, then hastily added. "Which is perfectly logical given its age and years of neglect." He didn't want to offend Cabot. In the past, he had inadvertently irritated people by being too candid.

"It's going to be a big deal to get this property into saleable condition." Cabot hesitated. "Mr. Winslow never really explained why you were coming."

Yates didn't think it was a secret. "I'm an authority on historical documents and books. I'm supposed to catalogue everything in the library and determine which items are potentially valuable."

"Well, good luck to you then. And I'd wear a dust mask if I was you. Some of those books haven't been touched since before I was born and that was longer ago than I care to remember."

"I thought that might be the case. I have some in my luggage."

"Well then, is there anything else I can help you with just at the moment?"

"Nothing comes to mind. I have the agency's number now."

Cabot pulled out a mildly incongruous business card. "That's my cell phone number, just in case. Good luck, Mr. Yates."

And a few moments later he was alone in the Winslow mansion.

He unpacked his clothing, which only half filled the commodious dresser in his room. Then he repeated the grand tour Cabot had provided, this time with the leisure to look at things he'd passed over the first time. Parts of the house were superficially clean, but even there he could see where the patina of the wood was overlaid with grime, and there was dust in places the cleaners had missed or ignored. The other parts of the mansion were so musty that he sneezed constantly on the third floor, and since neither it nor the fourth were in use, he went no further. He was interested in the master bedroom and spent some time there with the flashlight that was a routine part of his work equipment. Diaries and journals often made his work much easier and they were often kept in the bedroom, but despite poking around quite thoroughly and raising a good deal of dust, Yates was satisfied that if there were such things, they were not kept there.

Hunger had asserted itself by then and a brief exploration of the kitchen turned up nothing that appealed to him. Cabot had mentioned that he'd purchased enough food to last for a few days but his taste did not tempt Yates' palate. Sliced bread and cold cuts, a carton of potato salad, and bacon and eggs did not constitute an actual meal as far as he was concerned.

It had not occurred to him that the lack of a vehicle would present a problem in Newport, but he had expected to be closer to things. It was a considerable walk to the nearest restaurant, a dimly lit place that he would have passed by if he hadn't already come so far. The food – he ordered an elaborate salad – was better than he expected and he took a copy of the takeout menu with him when he left. There was a convenience store across the street and he picked up enough food for a day or two. Food was simply fuel as far as he was concerned, and a salami sandwich was just as adequate as a lobster dinner. He also noted a small laundry.

Yates spent the afternoon and most of the evening doing what he thought of as a preliminary survey. This consisted of mapping out where things were – or seemed to be – on a pad of lined paper. The library was erratically laid out with dead ends and twists and turns that were bewildering and he put off trying to create a detailed map, but the books were otherwise shelved in a logical manner, alphabetical by author within subject matter. There did not appear to be any fiction. A good many of the books were not in English. He could deal with Latin and German quite readily, French, Spanish, and Italian with some effort, but Greek was beyond his capacity, as was a small section which he believed to be Chinese.

Cabot had assured him that the attic was completely empty, not even a squirrel in residence, and had shown him the door to the basement, which led down from the kitchen. "There's a good deal of junk down there and you're welcome to look, but it's pretty filthy and the lights don't work." Yates had made a brief foray with his flashlight, but the surprisingly small basement – only half the size of the ground floor – contained only moldering furniture, rusting tools, and the heating system, which had been converted to gas from oil at some point. Two enormous oil tanks stood reproachfully empty in one corner.

He was quite fatigued by the time he retreated to his room that evening and added some notes to the file on his laptop. He had done some research on Otis Winslow as soon as he had accepted the job, although there wasn't a great deal to learn. Born in 1920, he had inherited the mansion and a mid-sized fortune while still in his twenties, had majored in comparative religion and philosophy at Miskatonic University, dabbled a bit in the business world but apparently more from a sense of duty than from any actual interest or aptitude.

He had married Emma Templeton Matheson in 1946. Their son Roger had been born in 1947 and Frederik in 1948. Emma passed away from cancer in 1954 and the boys had been sent off to a boarding school shortly thereafter. Otis had turned reclusive and while he supported both sons through their college careers, he rarely if ever had any direct contact with them. Arthur Winslow had alluded to this during one of their conversations. "There was some kind of estrangement between my father and grandfather. He rarely spoke of him. I suppose he never really knew him."

Otis pretty much vanished from public view during the late 1950s. He no longer attended social functions, hired people to administer his finances, and acquired the reputation of a recluse and an eccentric. Just over a year earlier, his cook – who had been away visiting her daughter for a week - had raised the alarm when she noticed that the larder was untouched and when he didn't appear for breakfast – she insisted that his habits were so regular that she could set her watch by them. She didn't venture up to his room herself; she had never been above the ground floor and didn't even know which was the master bedroom. The police had found the body.

The room was slightly chilly but Yates decided to forego the heater in favor of the thick pile of blankets on the bed. It was all quite comfortable and he expected to fall asleep immediately, but in that he was disappointed. For one thing, the house was far from silent. There were the usual creaks and groans that one expected in an old house that had begun to settle into its dotage, but they seemed louder, crisper, and closer than usual. There was a faint rasp that came every half minute or so, possibly a branch brushing against the side of the house, and it was so regular than Yates found himself waiting expectantly for its recurrence.

Once or twice he thought he heard the skittering of claws across a hard surface, but this seemed to originate outside the window and he decided it was another branch. At one point he could have sworn that he had heard a door close softly. He had sat up in bed that time, listening intently for any other sound. None had been forthcoming. Since he was not inclined to investigate – he would find nothing, of course, which would similarly prove nothing and reassure him not at all – he contented himself with checking to make sure he had locked the door to his room and then placed a chair in front of it so that it could not be opened without alerting him. Then he returned to bed, feeling a bit foolish.

The noises diminished after that, or perhaps he just grew accustomed to them. In any case, he found himself relaxing and prepared to sleep. But it was a long time coming and even after he finally dropped off, he woke three times in the night with his heart racing and his forehead sweaty. He could not remember dreaming and the house had been quiet on each occasion, so he had no idea what might have interrupted his sleep.

It was cold enough in the morning that he wore a sweater when he descended to the kitchen and made himself a light breakfast. He had already decided upon a plan of attack. The bulk of the papers were already in the library, with others in the kitchen, in a small table on the first floor landing, and in a narrow room facing the rear of the property whose function Yates was unable to determine but which he thought of as the lounge. He glanced through the kitchen paperwork while he was eating and determined that they were household related, mostly lists of groceries that had been delivered to the house or purchased separately by the cook, Mrs. Gordon from 1995 onward, a Mrs. Gibson prior to 1995. There was nothing of consequence among them.

The cache of paperwork on the landing was only slightly more promising. There was a ledger detailing household expenditures summarily, including payments to Gibson and Gordon, as well as a few other names that Yates didn't recognize. There were also property tax and utility bills, but nothing related to income taxes, which were presumably handled by Winslow's lawyers and/or accountants. Yates dismissed these as well.

The lounge proved more interesting. There were several letters – not all written in English – most relatively recent although he found one dated 1998. These would need to be examined more carefully, although they were not likely to be as significant as those in the library. He also found an estimate for some carpentry and masonry to be done in the library, with drawings, a bill of materials, and associated matters, all from the late 1980s, but they were incomplete and he couldn't figure out what the project consisted of. During his survey the previous day, Yates had seen correspondence from as far back as the 1940s in the library, which was much more likely to be of interest. He retrieved a cardboard box from the kitchen and transferred all the paperwork from the lounge into the box, which he carefully labeled before carrying it to the library and setting it down on the floor beside the desk.

Yates had felt a change the moment he had entered the room. It was an unsettling nerviness somewhere between excitement and apprehension. He had been enthusiastic about some of his jobs in the past, but had never previously experienced this intensity of anticipation. He paused for a moment or two, trying to decide why his reaction was so atypical this time. It was almost as though it was being imposed from without, which was naturally impossible. Eventually he decided to ignore the sensation and just do his job.

The morning passed quickly as he set about triaging the documents. The inconsequential stack was quite small – a few random bills, some newspaper clippings, letters from Winslow's financial managers with what appeared to be routine reports or inquiries. Yates placed these in a corner where they would be out of the way. It was more difficult to distinguish between the clearly and potentially interesting documents that remained. There were hundreds of letter from scores of correspondents. Only a small fraction were more recent than 2000 and the bulk fell between 1947 and 1984, with a handful between that point and the end of the century. He finally decided to leave all the correspondence together rather than choose an arbitrary point of bifurcation.

There were no journals to be found, which was rather disappointing. Yates did separate occasional single sheets of paper upon which journal style notations were made. As was the case with the bulk of the correspondence, the notes dealt primarily with arcane religious matters. Winslow had been thoroughly ecumenical. Even during his brief scrutiny, Yates had seen references to a variety of creeds, not all of which he recognized. Some even embraced occult concepts including out of body experiences, mind reading, and reincarnation. He remembered noticing an impressive selection of books on similar subjects during his quick survey of the library. Winslow apparently never abandoned his interest in the subject following his college days.

There were charts and diagrams among the papers, some with unrecognizable symbols, some printed and some drawn by hand. Yates was confident that many of these were astrological in nature. One of his previous jobs had been to evaluate the estate of a professional astrologer who had once advised a President of the United States and more than one member of Congress. He tried to separate these into their own pile, but often the same charts contained other symbols or notations that Yates didn't recognize. He made a mental note to glance through the occult book section to see if he could determine their relevance.

He also accumulated a very large pile of loose papers upon which mathematical equations had been scrawled. A few had annotations including "too many variables," "faulty mechanics," or "promising, but incomplete." He would list them as a single entry rather than individually. It seemed highly unlikely that they had any significance, and in any case he lacked the training to evaluate or even understand the mathematics.

Yates had a late lunch after having finished his preliminary sorting of the paperwork. The next step would be a more metaphysical rearrangement. He would have to go through the library, shelf by shelf, and note which books were obviously or potentially valuable and which were not. It was obviously impractical to physically segregate them, so he would first half to assign a designation for each aisle - a letter of the alphabet would serve the purpose – and a particular shelf – each assigned a separate number. Shelf D6, therefore, might contain Gridley's *History of the Dissenters*, first edition, plus two or three titles that might possibly have antiquarian value, plus a dozen books unlikely to be worth anything appreciable.

With a sandwich in one hand, Yates walked through the library hoping to determine a layout pattern, some logical arrangement that would facilitate his work. It was not as simple as it seemed. The library was such a maze, and so poorly lit, that he became disoriented more than once, and when he tried to retrace his path he found himself in an aisle he had not previously entered. Arthur Winslow had told him there were ten thousand books in the library. His first walk through had convinced Yates that the real number was twice that, and now he believed that his estimate had still been far too low.

He made his way back to the desk, took up a clipboard with a pad of legal sized paper, and slipped a pack of three by five cards and a roll of tape into his pocket. Then he went to the closest shelf and taped a card to one end, marking it with the letter "A". He drew a small rectangle on the top sheet of his pad, and moved on to the next.

The mapping and labeling consumed most of the afternoon, which was about twice as long as he had expected. The last card he placed bore the letters "AV", which meant that he had mapped forty-eight aisles. Part of the delay was because he had needed to redo his map five times. He kept finding new aisles in sections that he had decided were completely mapped, which forced him to redraw that section and the ways in which it all interconnected. Even at the end, he had only decided that he was done because he hadn't stumbled into an unlabeled section for a while. It was quite possible that around some corner that he hadn't noticed lay an entirely new stretch of shelving. But at least he had enough of the groundwork laid that he could start evaluating the contents of the library. He had been experiencing the oddest feeling that he was not alone for some time now, and he actually went around checking that the doors were all secured. Reassured if not satisfied, he returned to the library.

His spreadsheets and database formats were all prepared. He had standardized both long since. He opened both of these on one laptop, then booted up the second and quickly opened multiple web pages. There was no such thing as a predetermined price on books like these, only a price range depending in part upon the conditions of the book and conditions of the market. Yates ignored the prices that dealers were asking. These were invariably inflated by wishful thinking. He was more interested in what dealers were willing to pay. Estates this size would not be interested in dealing with scores of buyers; they would want the books disposed of quickly and in lots.

Yates went to work.

He spent four hours doing searches on the web and entering information into his database, occasionally consulting his map so that he could re-examine a particular title in order to refine his description of its condition or to confirm details that showed up during the searches. There was only one occasion upon which he was disoriented and he found an error on his map, which was very strange because he had been very careful while working on the layout. It was almost as if part of the library had rearranged itself when he wasn't looking. It wasn't until later that he considered the possibility that someone had simply moved a couple of his index cards.

Although he planned to work through the evening, he decided that a short break would be refreshing. The weather was pleasant so he walked down to the diner and had another surprisingly good meal. When he returned to the mansion, he still wasn't quite ready to go back to work so he chose instead to explore the grounds.

Hedges and shrubbery had spread in every direction like barbarian hordes but he could still make out much of the layout of the gardens, mostly because of stone walls, statuary, a very overgrown fountain, and two gazebos, both weathered and unstable. It took better than half an hour to completely circumnavigate the building and he was slightly out of breath and footsore by the time he reached the front door again. There had been a service entrance in the rear but his key had not fit the lock. He was somewhat thoughtful when his exploration was done. The foundation suggested that there was a full basement, but the space he had examined was about half that size. A call to Cabot was in order, but it could wait until the next day.

His evening was uneventful, save for a return of the sense that he was being watched, but he shook it off and continued to work. Eventually the inadequate rest he had managed the previous night overcame his good intentions and after finding himself nodding off, Yates shut everything down and made his way back to his room. It was warm enough that he didn't even consider turning on the heater and he undressed quickly and went immediately to bed, and to sleep.

It was just after midnight when he woke up. He glanced at his travel clock automatically even as he was trying to decide just what it was that had disturbed his sleep. The house was presently as quiet as it always was. As long as he was awake, Yates decided to empty his bladder. The bathroom was down the hall – only the master bedroom had a private one – and he put on his dressing gown and slippers. Mission accomplished, he was on his way back to his room when he heard a sound from the ground floor. It wasn't threatening, not exactly, but it was inexplicable. It sounded as though someone was sliding a heavy piece of furniture across the floor. Yates was not a timid man, but neither was he foolhardy. He retrieved his flashlight from his room, and an iron from the fireplace, before descending to investigate. The sound had only lasted about ten seconds and nothing had happened since. Making as little sound as possible, Yates explored all of the ground floor rooms, leaving the library for the last. As far as he could determine, nothing was out of place, and certainly there was no sign of an intruder. The outer doors were both locked.

His pulse was racing when he entered the library, but all seemed equally quiet there. The lights were, as always, inadequate and seemed to cast so many sinister shadows that Yates thought he might be better off with his flashlight alone. Despite his trepidation, however, he found the desk just as he had left it. The rows of shelving were so extensive and idiosyncratic that he supposed that a half dozen intruders could have eluded him, but the sense that he was not alone had faded and he began to feel rather silly. His mind might well have misinterpreted some perfectly ordinary sound. After a cursory search, he returned to his bed, telling himself he was being very immature, but once again he locked his door and blockaded it with a chair.

He woke the following morning feeling quite refreshed and when he remembered his alarm in the middle of the night, he felt more than slightly embarrassed. He finished off the bacon and eggs Cabot had left for him and then called the agent's number and asked him if there was a second staircase to the basement. It was only later that he realized it was Saturday and that he was probably bothering the man on his own time.

"Not that I know of. I've been through the house pretty thoroughly and haven't seen any doors that I haven't opened."

Yates explained about the disparity in the size of the basement. "I don't know anything about that, Mr. Yates. I suppose we could try to dig up the original plans for the building."

"That might be wise, if it isn't a major project. If Winslow closed off part of the basement for some reason, we ought to know."

"It might have been seepage. The ground is pretty porous around there. Easier to close it off than try to keep it dry."

Cabot promised to look into it, but he didn't sound enthusiastic.

Yates set to work but after a couple of hours he realized that his attention was wandering. At first he couldn't figure out what was bothering him and he tried to concentrate, but after another half hour he knew what the problem was. Cabot's explanation about the truncated basement was unsatisfactory.

He set his work aside, telling himself that he needed a break in any case. Then he went back down into the basement and paced off its length, then returned to the ground floor and carefully counted his steps. The last one was a pace or too short of where the library wall stood. That mean that if there was any surviving entrance to the rest of the basement, it was probably hidden somewhere among the stacks.

In his earlier excursions he had paid no attention to the floor, which he now observed was fashioned of intricately intertwined ovals and ellipses and curved pieces that had no individual names, all white or sand colored. There was a word for this and it took him a few minute to dredge it up out of his mind. Marquetry. There was no pattern that he could detect; every swath of floor was entirely different. The only actual walls were the exterior ones and he had not seen anything suggesting an old door. A dozen or more supporting columns were distributed – presumably in orderly rows although Yates was never able to see more than one at a time – but none were thick enough to conceal even an artfully disguised accessway.

Yates spent the better part of an hour looking for a trapdoor before deciding that he was being foolish and returning to his work.

It was almost dusk when a thought occurred to him. Among the papers he had deemed of little potential value had been correspondence relating to alterations in the library. He sorted through that pile until he found the documents he remembered and read through them. The work in question was apparently completed during the fall of 1987 to the satisfaction of Otis Winslow, who had paid promptly. There was an acknowledgment from the project management firm which had coordinated the work. There were also a few drawings, each numbered, but there was no legend to identify what they were. Yates knew very little about such things, but he recognized a wiring diagram and a sketch of a spiral staircase which resembled nothing he had seen in the house. There was no mention of it in the other paperwork.

One drawing did stand out, so odd that he would have thought it unrelated if it had not been stapled to a list of measurements that was paper clipped to a bill of materials. At first he thought it was a stylized sunburst, a circular central body with eight exactly equal extrusions like tentacles, each fitting into the next so that they formed a solid though irregular shape. A large open eye, lidless, was drawn in its exact center. If he was reading the list of measurements correctly, it would have been just over two feet in diameter.

And it looked familiar.

He had seen it earlier that same day, when he'd been searching the library. It was part of the marquetry. But just where he had seen it, he really couldn't say

Yates told himself that he should get back to work, but instead he changed the batteries in his flashlight – the old ones had started to fade noticeably – and began exploring the library once again. It didn't take long to find what he was looking for.

The eight armed figure was at the intersection of two aisles, perfectly centered, and now that he looked at it, Yates wondered why he hadn't found it remarkable the first time he had seen it. It was at least five times as big as any other segment of the mosaic, and it had a darker color, a kind of greenish brown, which appeared nowhere else on the floor. He crouched beside it, rubbed his chin, then began rapping the floor. He wasn't sure what he should be listening for, but in movies they always did that when they were looking for secret passages. It should sound hollow, shouldn't it? But as far as he could tell there was no auditory difference between this and any other section of the floor.

He tried all the predictable things. None of the recesses were large enough for him to insert his fingers, so he could not pull it up. Jumping up and down on the center had no effect except to make him short of breath and a precariously shelved book shook itself loose and fell to the floor with a thud that startled him disproportionately. He could not detect any secret switches hidden on the shelving units and he was nowhere near any of the outer walls. There was no cavity where a key might be inserted and no scrape marks to suggest the entire piece might turn in place. Yates finally abandoned his investigation in part because he had no more ideas and in part because the uncanny feeling that he was not alone had returned.

Although he had planned to work into the evening, he shut own both computers and left the library, closing the doors behind him for the first time since he had arrived. He felt a sudden antipathy toward his surroundings so he found his wallet and then left the house, walking briskly toward the downtown lights.

The diner was closed but he hadn't planned to stop there anyway. Although not a heavy drinker, neither was Yates an abstainer. He found a restaurant – The Red Schooner – that wasn't too crowded, and found himself eating fish and chips and drinking Pinot Grigio. He hadn't realized how tense he was until the muscles in his back and neck started to relax, but he attributed this to his admittedly unergonomic work habits rather than the atmosphere of the mansion. He had a second glass of wine with his meal, which was unusual, and a third with desert, which was unheard of. After all, he wasn't driving.

Yates neither stumbled nor staggered on his way back, even though it was dark and the streets were not well lit in that part of the city. He did, however, walk with exaggerated care and it took three tries to get his key into the front door.

The alcohol dulled his senses because he was about to start up the stairs before he noticed anything. The nature of the sensation eluded him at first but after he paused for a few seconds, it felt like the air around him was charged with electricity. Some primal instinct told him that it centered on the library so he crossed to the doors and pulled them open. It was pitch dark inside but he caught the slightest suggestion of movement just before he turned on the lights. At the corner of his vision, a shadow moved at the far end of the nearest aisle of books, gone so quickly that he thought he might have imagined it. There was a faint scratching sound, one he had heard before, but it too ceased before he could really concentrate.

He started forward, intending to investigate, but caution finally triumphed over befuddled bravado and instead he stopped. It was not the first time he had been unsettled by something in the mansion, but it was the first time that he felt actively afraid. Gathering his wits, he backed to the door, turned out the lights, and closed the library up behind him. The only reason he didn't run up to his room is that he didn't feel steady enough.

In the morning, however, he just felt embarrassed. Fortunately no one had seen his retreat into what he thought of as hysteria. In the daylight, the mansion was far less formidable. He peeked into the library on the way to breakfast – he had forgotten to resupply so it was toast and coffee only – but nothing appeared to be amiss. He did take a cursory look through the stacks while the laptops were booting up, but he didn't penetrate even as far as the elaborate inlaid piece he had examined the previous day. Yates did notice a mistake in his map, however; he had missed one aisle between H and I, although for some reason he had labeled it as S. He decided he must not have been paying attention.

There was no rule – not even a personal one – that he had to finish up one category of material before starting the next, although that was usually his modus operandi, but he decided to spend the day going through documents rather than books. If this resulted from a subconscious impulse not to penetrate into the maze of shelves, he did not allow that fact to impinge on his awareness. Nor did he spend any time wondering how he could have mislabeled a shelf and then failed to notice it later. He had examined three books from shelf S already.

Yates found Winslow's personal correspondence a bit daunting. Normally he would have arranged the letters chronologically by correspondent, but even though he had considerable difficulty following much of their abstruse content, it was evident that in large part they constituted a single conversation among many parties. Winslow had been one of the central figures of that intercourse but perhaps not the only one. There were also significant gaps at times but he was unable to determine whether that had been a lapse in the discussion or whether other documents were missing. He did find a tantalizing paragraph in which one Viktor Lorenz of Prague included the statement: "I assume that you have documented the auditory phenomena in your journal." This suggested that Winslow had in fact kept more formal records, although he had no idea where they might be.

He used his cell phone to order a pizza and a soft drink and sat on the front steps to wait for them. Two things seemed to be missing at the Winslow mansion – the old man's journals and the other half of the basement. It seemed likely that the two were linked. He wondered if he could talk Arthur Winslow into breaking through the floor – or better yet the interior basement wall - to investigate. It seemed unlikely. The heir was in a hurry to tie up the loose ends, sell off the valuable contents and then the property itself. Expensive renovations other than those required to meet code would have no place in his game plan.

The delivery man was tall and skinny and looked to be about twenty. He was also chatty.

"Are you the new owner?"

Yates shook his head. "Just an employee. I'll be here a couple of weeks though so you might see me again."

"Better you than me."

Yates raised an eyebrow. "What's the matter? Does the place have a bad reputation? It's not supposed to be haunted, is it?"

'Nah, no ghosts. But people around here just don't like the place. Some of them say it makes their skin crawl when they drive by."

"Did you know old man…Mr. Winslow? The former owner. Ever deliver him a pizza?"

"Not pizza, but when I was in high school I used to deliver groceries for the IGA. Mostly shut-ins. Mrs. Gordon used to order for him. She was okay but she never let me go anywhere except the kitchen. I don't think she spent much time in the rest of the house either. And she told me they couldn't keep a steady cleaning person so they had to hire a service."

"Did she say why?"

He shrugged. "Some houses just feel bad. That's all she would say."

"I don't suppose you'd know how I could get in touch with her? I have some questions she might be able to answer."

"No, sorry."

Yates was determined to get some work done that evening and attacked the next stack of documents energetically if not enthusiastically. He finished that lot and then another, finding nothing of interest except a couple of random letters from the 1970s. One was in Russian, which he didn't speak, and one that he thought might be a Scandinavian language, although the first page was missing so there was no return address. He set these aside.

He had just sorted out a third lot when he caught himself yawning and decided that he'd done enough for the day. He stood and stretched and as he did so he heard a thump, exactly as though a book had fallen from its place on a shelf. With his flashlight in hand, he started along a path he had pretty well memorized, but he must have slipped up somewhere because he became disoriented after a moment or two. Having decided that the fallen book could stay where it was until he happened on it in the normal course of events, he started to make his way back toward the front of the library.

The next intersection was a familiar one. The elaborate eight-tentacled pattern was just as he remembered it. There was a puzzle here as well. It was the most brightly lit portion of the stacks and he returned the flashlight to his pocket. For the first time he looked up and contemplated the lighting fixtures. They were all mounted high enough that the bulbs could not be changed without fetching something upon which to stand. This was necessary because the shelves themselves were so tall. They created artificial canyons into which only a small fraction of the light was diffracted. This intersection was directly under one of the fixtures, so it was quite well illuminated. It was also the only light that had a pull cord.

Curious, Yates reached up and pulled the chain. The light went out, unsurprisingly. It wasn't completely dark because the others all stayed on but it fell like a dark blanket over the intersection. And then something began to glow.

Yates crouched and stared at the floor. Numerals were now visible, each a single digit, one on each of the tentacles. They ran from two through nine. A slightly larger number one shimmered in the exact center of the figure. He stood up and turned the light back on. The numbers disappeared immediately. When he turned the light off a second time, they reappeared. Yates ran his hand over them but they were not raised or recessed surfaces. Whatever was glowing was embedded inside the floor piece itself.

Although he was pretty certain that this had to be a bizarre kind of combination lock, he had no idea how to operate it. His statistical skills were not up to computing the value of nine factorial in his head, but he knew there had to be tens of millions of combinations. Had he seen anything that might help? Nothing came to mind. But he might have passed the combination by without recognizing its significance, if it was around to be found at all. If this really was what he thought it might be.

Yates had a lot to think about when he went to bed, but neither that nor the odd sounds in the night were enough to disturb his sleep, although he did toss a bit during the ten seconds when something very heavy began moving on the ground floor.

He put in a full day of work on Monday, broken only by a mid-day break for a sandwich and some groceries. It would not be fair to say that he had dismissed the puzzle in the library completely from his mind, but he was able to mentally set it aside for further examination later. He was, after all, being paid for a specific job, not to explore mysteries that were none of his business. On the other hand, if there was some way of entering the other half of the basement, it was entirely possible that there were materials there which did relate to his duties.

That night he was woken by a repeat of the scratching sound that he had heard on his first day. It could not have lasted more than a few seconds, but he was alert and sitting upright before it had finished. There was no question that it originated inside the house. Although he told himself to ignore it and go back to sleep, Yates found himself out of bed and into his slippers almost without thinking about it. He felt foolish about taking the fireplace iron again, but the flashlight was indispensible.

He was quite certain that the sound had come from the library and in fact when he approached it – he had left the doors open – he fancied her heard a faint scratching sound in the distance. He was reminded of the scuttling of crabs across stone. The library lights came up as soon as he touched the switch, but even in the daylight they did very little to relieve the gloom except where the massive desk stood. Yates cast his eyes over the paperwork he had left there and two good sized stacks of books, but as far as he could tell nothing had been disturbed. His laptops were powered down and closed.

He moved across the open space with exaggerated caution. His working hypothesis was that some animal had found its way into the house, probably a raccoon since the disturbances had come after the fall of night. Although he had a vague recollection that raccoons were sometimes rabid, he thought that what he had heard was too tentative to be the actions of a deranged animal. Moving horizontally along the first rank of shelves, he swept his light around at each opening before proceeding. Nothing seemed to be out of the ordinary.

Exploring further was more problematic. The layout was full of dead ends and idiosyncratic turns that made any systematic approach impossible. Yates decided to change tactics. He chose an aisle at random and walked briskly forward, whistling loudly. If it was an animal, this might well send it into panicky flight, which would reveal its location. If it was some odd auditory artifact of the house itself, nothing would happen.

Nothing happened, or at least, nothing seemed to have happened.

Yates had wandered about for a few minutes, but his whistle had gone dry and he was feeling more than slightly foolish. He peered around, trying to orient himself, then started back toward the library entrance. After only one foray into a dead end, he caught sight of the desk ahead of him and emerged from the stacks, anxious to get back to bed. But the night had one more surprise in store for him.

The desk stood exactly where it should be, but he was quite sure that when he had stopped work for the day, the books had been piled up to his right and the carton of documents to his left. They had been similarly placed when he entered the library on his apparently futile quest. But now they had been swapped around. Otherwise, everything appeared to be untouched.

Yates exited from the library hastily and made certain the doors were securely shut before retreating to his room. He slept uneasily.

They say everything looks brighter in the daylight, but his nerves were so on edge the following morning that he stood in front of the closed doors with his arms crossed, considering calling Arthur Winslow and explaining that his health had taken a bad turn and that he would not be able to continue with the cataloguing. Two things prevented him from doing so immediately. The first was that he had never voluntarily abandoned a project – he had once stopped work when an interim check bounced. It was a matter of pride to him as well as a marketable commodity. There was limited demand for his particular expertise and having a reputation for reliability was important.

The second thing was that he had a sudden burst of inspiration. He thought that he just might have figured out the combination to the tentacled lock, if that's what it really was. He glanced up at the date inscribed above the doorway and memorized it. But before he acted upon it, someone knocked at the door. He opened it to find three women standing there looking at him suspiciously.

"We come for Mr. Cabot," said one with a heavy Portuguese accent.

"You must be the cleaning people. Come in, please. I haven't seen Mr. Cabot this morning." In fact, the man hadn't been to the house at all, he realized, which seemed odd.

The woman looked uncertain but she seemed to accept the situation readily. The three of them went inside. Yates felt obligated to remain accessible while they cleaned the kitchen and ground floor bathroom and vacuumed the front hall. Apparently the bedrooms were not part of their weekly schedule because they packed up as soon as they were done. Yates saw them out and closed the door, then quickly went to the library.

The items on the desk were back the way he had left them.

Yates frowned, wondering if he had been mistaken the night before. Or had he even come downstairs? Might it all have been an elaborate dream? He had experienced lucid dreams in the past. But if that was the case, how had the library doors been closed?

Whatever trepidation he might have felt was drowned by his excitement. His idea was probably wrong, but his instincts rarely let him down. He found a scrap of paper on the desk and wrote a sequence of numbers: 12161987. Then he walked into the stacks.

As though fate were leading the way, Yates went directly to the right intersection. He stood staring down at the floor for a few seconds, then pulled down the cord to the light. It went off and the nine numbers were illuminated again. Crouching, he realized that even if he had the right combination, he had no idea how to enter it. Pressing down on the individual tentacles had no effect. They could not be pushed or pulled or turned or raised or depressed. A momentary doubt twisted his face, but then he reached out and tapped the "1" and then the "2" and continued until he had finished the sequence.

Initially it did not appear to have had any effect. Perhaps the mechanism had become stuck over the course of years or perhaps it took a while for the input to be verified. In any case, Yates was about to give up and go back to work when the numbers abruptly disappeared even though he had not turned the light back on. The entire circular design had begun to glow, and there was the faintest of hissing sounds, like escaping air. Yates took a step backward, startled despite his anticipation that something like this might happen, and then the hatchway in the floor opened up.

It was bizarre. Yates would have sworn that it was all a single piece of fused stone, but the tentacles disengaged and opened like the petals of a flower. The main body dropped out of sight, but he could see where it was hinged and connected to the adjacent flooring. There was nothing but darkness within the hole at first, but then it began to lighten and flicker and he realized that a succession of electric lights was being activated beneath the floor. Cautiously, he peered over the rim and saw the top of a spiral staircase. There was no doubt in his mind now. He had found the secret way into the basement.

It took some care to lower himself down onto the top step, which was well below the floor itself, because the opening was quite narrow. He had to crouch until he was a bit lower but then he made his way expeditiously to the bottom. The railing was wrought iron but the staircase wound around a supporting central pillar of concrete once he was halfway down. The basement had been finished off; he could see paneling immediately and flooring a few seconds later. He reached the bottom and looked around.

It was a large, rectangular space, of course. The staircase was very close to the wall that divided the basement in half. That wall was covered with shelves that were half filled with books, half filled with odds and ends that he didn't immediately recognize. The opposite wall was mostly bare and it was white plaster rather than paneling. An interwoven series of tubes and wires had a major junction at the far left, rose slowly to a second junction at the top, descended symmetrically to a third on the right, and then dropped to the final at floor level in the very center before looping back up to the left. The open space was therefore a very large oval.

But what really dominated the space was an impressively large, enigmatic machine that stood squarely in the center of the space. It was about fifteen feet long and half that in width, stood slightly taller than Yates, and seemed to be constructed primarily of brass and copper. There were dials and levers and gauges and buttons sprinkled liberally across its surface. A good sized, utilitarian desk stood nearby with a single wooden chair. Yates walked slowly around the machine and saw that a thick sheaf of copper tubing and rubber coated wires ran out of the far end of the machine and terminated at the leftmost junction on the rear wall. There were labels on most of the controls – several on/off switches, focusing, computation, feedback, gauss, variation, interface, rotation, alignment, insertion, and so on, but none of them told him the purpose of the machine.

He rested a hand on it. The metal was cold and there was nothing to suggest that it was operating. At the far end he found two portable generators but they were also powered down. There was dust, but not as much as he would have expected if this place had been abandoned for years. Otis Winslow, or someone else, had been using this room at least until quite recently.

Yates grew even more excited when he approached the shelves. The first books that caught his eye were arranged together. *De Vermis Myteriis* was not new to him; he had found one in reasonable condition in the collection of another client a few years earlier. But he had never seen an actual *Necronomicon* except through a glass window when he'd visited the library at Miskatonic University as an undergraduate, and that copy had mysteriously disappeared later that same year.

He took that volume down and carefully opened it, just to make sure it was the real thing. The book plate inside told him that he was holding the same one that had been purloined decades earlier. Arthur Winslow would not be happy about that, but Yates' code of ethics would not allow him to remain silent about his discovery. The other books on that particular shelf were not all familiar to him, and several were not in English, but they all seemed to concern the occult.

Those of the shelf below were much newer but in his case they were nearly as arcane. Some dealt with mathematics on a level that was completely impenetrable to him. Some were discussions of quantum physics. There was a large *Manual of Statistical Analysis* and a slender *Treatise on the Possibility of Multiple Realities*; the latter appeared to be a bound but unpublished doctoral thesis.

He was even more excited when he saw what was on the third and fourth shelves. They were slender volumes and each spine bore only a number. They were in order from 1945 through 2014. In several instances there were two with the same date. Apparently Winslow had had a lot to say in those years, which were mostly in the 1950s and 1970s. Yates took down the earliest one and opened it, confirming that it was in fact a journal, relieved to see that Winslow had a very clear cursive handwriting.

Setting the journal back in place, he spent a few minutes examining the other articles on the shelves. A few were arcane pieces of electronics which he passed over quickly. Others were just odd and almost random. There was a glass vial filled with very fine sand. It stood near a gnarled piece of wood that had very horny protrusions. It was so dark that he thought at first that it had been burnt, but when he picked it up there was no sign of charring. In fact it felt rather oily. There was a pale green crystal formation the size of a baseball that looked as though it might have been part of a coral reef and a dead beetle of some sort mounted inside a glass box. It had eight legs and a fierce looking head and was not of a species he recognized. But he was not a naturalist.

He tried the desk next. There was an open journal dated 2015 but only a single entry.

I am feeling increasingly unwell and do not believe I can maintain my vigil much longer. I have known all along that I should have made provision for a successor, but my reluctance to share my discoveries has become a part of what I am. And frankly I have little interest in the consequences once I am gone. In fact, my greatest regret is that I will be unable to observe them.

The desk drawers were empty except for some ball point pens, a blank pad of paper, a box of old fashioned glass tube fuses, a bottle of aspirin, two pairs of canvas work gloves, and several empty bottles with screw top lids. There was a large wooden box beside the desk that contained a shovel, a hoe, a butterfly net, a long plastic ladle, a pair of tongs, and a wire basket.

Finally he walked down to the far wall and examined the oval and its outline of tubes and wires. Heavy brackets held everything in place. Nothing here was labeled clearly but each tube was a different color, and the wiring all had metal tags with short serial numbers. He could not find any breaks anywhere, or any place where another piece of equipment might have been attached. Some white sand had been spilled on the floor along the edge of the room, but less than a handful.

Yates searched a bit longer without turning anything up of interest, then scooped up an armful of journals – the oldest ones – and carried them upstairs. He felt an uncanny reluctance to read them in the basement.

The earliest journals were filled with anecdotes about his wife and less frequently his children. Although Otis expressed mild pride in his offspring, there were hints of irritation at how much of his wife's time they consumed. That he was in love with her was evident; it was almost an obsession and he wrote at least a few lines about her nearly every day. Yates felt somewhat voyeuristic reading them, but reminded himself that both husband and wife were dead now. The two boys as well.

Since Otis did not need to work, and probably had no aptitude for practical matters, he devoted his time to study. His college career had been in comparative religion and philosophy and his interest sharpened rather than declined. He taught himself several languages so that he could correspond with people scattered all over the world and by the early 1950s he was in touch with people from Tibet, India, Europe, and Africa. Although there was no indication that he had ever written anything for publication, the accounts in the journals suggested that he was taken seriously by a number of prominent people in that field.

Winslow was also something of a mathematics prodigy. This was less obvious because he rarely wrote about it, and when he did Yates usually could not follow what he was saying. The last journal he had brought upstairs was 1953 and at that point Winslow appeared to be a remarkably happy, self satisfied, high intelligent man, although possibly something of a recluse already. Fortunately his wife did not care to travel either, or at least that's what Winslow believed.

It was well after noon so Yates prepared himself a meal – sandwiches again – and wrestled with an ethical problem while he ate. It did not appear that the journals were going to do much to advance his work and he did not feel justified in being paid to satisfy his curiosity. On the other hand, the machine in the basement could conceivably have some value and at worst he could report to his employer that he had found the secret entrance to the hidden room. He compromised by telling himself that if he didn't find anything of value in the journals by the end of the day, he would return to cataloguing and pass on the information to Arthur Winslow. Let him make the decision regarding future investigation.

He replaced the volumes he had abstracted and carried 1954 through 1963 upstairs.

Emma Winslow died in 1954 after a protracted and debilitating illness. The journal entries were much shorter during this period and ceased entirely for several weeks following her death. By the end of the year both boys had been sent off to a boarding school and their names never reappeared in any of the entries. It was as though they had died as well, or perhaps Otis had only seen them as extensions of his wife, purposeless once she was gone.

The entries began to lengthen again toward the end of the year. There were several allusions to the resumption of his correspondence. Sometimes the entries were very technical, but Yates learned that by the following year Winslow had decided to bring his two remaining passions together. He was going to convert all religious tenets to mathematical expressions and then create a kind of unified field theory of religion.

It was also evident that he had lost his faith. There was nothing to indicate that Winslow had belonged to any recognized sect although he had been nominally Christian, and he had clearly believed that there was a superior being, if not a creator. His vision of that being had changed radically, however.

By the end of the 1950s, Winslow had apparently alienated a number of his correspondents and replaced them with new ones. The entries were much longer – sometimes a single entry covered a score of pages – and they became more abstruse. Yates struggled with the strange nomenclature and understood only a fraction of what he was reading, but a general sense of the changes in Winslow came through. He had not abandoned his intention to analyze religion mathematically, but he had expanded his definition to include the occult. Yates kept expecting to read that Winslow hoped to contact his dead wife, but that never seemed to be a part of his plan. It was God, or at least some superior being, whom Winslow hoped to communicate with.

Toward the end of 1959 he started building something he called the Interpreter. His descriptions were vague but it was clearly a machine of some sort and Yates had no doubt that what he'd seen in the basement was the device itself or some later iteration of it. Winslow only hinted at its purpose which was to "process the equations as they are refined." Yates had begun skipping the entries that contained large mathematical expressions, but even if he had read them all, he would not have understood their meaning.

The next two years' worth of entries were relatively dull. Winslow would be excited about a small success one day and devastated by a setback on the next. Late in 1962 he contemplated abandoning the project, but instead dismantled the Interpreter and started over again. The following year he was clearly more hopeful, and in July one of his entries contained a paragraph that Yates read several times.

The suggestions from Gephardt have proved most helpful. Although I am still unable to pierce the veil even visually, it was quite clear during the morning's session that I have tapped into the integument. Feedback began to rise and continued until it exceeded the level of power drawn. I feared that it was an instrumentation problem rather than an actual breakthrough, so I cut all power to the Interpreter. It continued to operate for almost ten minutes before abruptly shutting down. Unfortunately, there was no visual, auditory, or tactile evidence.

Had Winslow been trying to develop a new power source of some kind? That wasn't even hinted at in the journals. Yates finished reading the entries for the year 1963. Winslow had become discouraged again over the course of the winter because he was unable to duplicate, let alone enhance, his single successful experiment. But just before Thanksgiving he had written another provocative statement.

I have acquired the book for which I have searched for so long. It has apparently passed through several hands since it was stolen from the university and I had despaired of ever discovering its whereabouts. But fortunately it was in the possession of a collector who recently died and whose sister and heir had no idea of its value. One of my agents was able to obtain it for a ridiculously low sum before she learned otherwise. I will begin to derive its equations tomorrow and incorporate them into the master theorem.

His back complained when he stood up and he was surprised to discover how late it was. Yates gathered up the journals and carried them downstairs. He was replacing them on their shelf when he suddenly had the feeling that he was being watched. It came upon him quite suddenly and intensely and he literally broke out in a cold sweat. Turning slowly, he let his eyes travel from one side of the open space to the other. There weren't many places where even a small animal could remain out of sight.

Taking a deep breath, he crossed quickly to the desk and took the hoe out of the wooden box. He wasn't afraid of rats – he'd encountered more than a few in his line of work – but this felt like something more substantial, more menacing. Raising the hoe to a striking position, he walked around the corner of the desk and assured himself that nothing was crouching there.

The machine – the Interpreter – was a different story. There was plenty of room to walk around it, but nothing to prevent someone or something else from moving ahead of him and remaining out of sight. He walked briskly back and forth past the nearest narrow end, but the space just beyond was obscured. So he walked completely around the machine, listening intently, but other than a muffled thump from somewhere above him in the library – another book falling over in all likelihood – there was nothing to hear.

The bad feeling did not go away. It existed outside of reason. Still carrying the hoe, he scooped up the next few journals with his free arm and walked over to the staircase. He left the hoe leaning against it as he scuttled up to the library

He felt a little better once the hatch was closed, but his pulse was still elevated. Yates wished he had picked up a bottle of wine, or better yet some rum, and he considered walking downtown to find a bar. But the lure of the journals was too strong, and after pacing back and forth for a bit to work off the tension, he sat down at the desk and opened 1964.

In May of 1964, Winslow recorded a breakthrough. By this point Yates had a vague idea of what he was trying to achieve. Winslow believed that the urge toward religion resulted from the human mind's peripheral awareness that reality was subjective. What people perceived as words from the gods were actually distorted interpretations of thoughts originating with beings that existed on a different plane of existence. He also believed that mathematics was the best language with which to describe the matrix of these various realities, and that by properly analyzing religious beliefs and reducing them to equations, he could distinguish among those realities and possibly even experience them with his own senses.

The Interpreter was a kind of computer built around a chamber of prisms, mirrors, and other devices which were designed to express visual images in what was effect a different natural language. These images were then projected onto a small screen mounted at one end of the machine, although Yates had observed no such feature during his examination. On evening in May, just as Winslow was about to end the day's experiments, the screen had grown momentarily cloudy and then, just for a second, displayed a barren landscape of rock and sand. It faded immediately and, despite several hours of tweaking, did not reappear. Winslow was elated rather than discouraged, however, because he had finally observed concrete evidence that he was not chasing a chimera.

Yates was inclined to dismiss it as a wish fulfillment hallucination, or perhaps the Interpreter had somehow picked up a television signal.

It was not until the following January that Winslow reported any further success.

The latest series of adjustments did the trick. I was able to acquire and hold the image for a full minute. Its appearance was the same as before – or at least very similar. It displays a stretch of desert, light colored sand pockmarked with dark, jagged rocks of various sizes. There is no sign of life, no movement at all. The sky appears somewhat dark but the focus is not fine enough to determine whether there are stars or other features. I need to design a larger display as soon as I have solved the tracking problem.

Most of the entries for the balance of that year and the first half of 1966 were so technical that Yates skimmed through them. Winslow reported recurrences of the desolate view, which apparently never changed in any discernible fashion, and gradually increased the length of time it would remain visible. Twice he referred to some book as being his Rosetta Stone but it wasn't until December that he identified it specifically as the *Necronomicon*. "I believe its author was naturally able to perceive what I can see only by means of the Interpreter. It is that faculty, perhaps, which led to his madness."

Advances came slowly, but Otis Winslow was a patient man. He built a larger screen which apparently had been placed on the desk in the basement. Yates had seen no sign of it during his search. The following year he was able to hold the image for as long as an hour, but could not always summon it when he wanted to. This he attributed to "friction among the planes" without explaining what that meant.

The next two years did not radically change the situation and the entries were much shorter. Yates thought he detected some exasperation in Winslow's notes, but if that was the case, it was not enough to disrupt his obsession. As the periods of observation grew longer and the picture more refined, Winslow reported that the landscape was not as static as he originally believed.

It is not a snapshot or a still life that I am seeing. Although there appears to be no life, that does not mean that there is no change. A small hillock of sand at the extreme right of the picture has grown slightly larger since I began observing, and the contour of a distant dune has changed its shape ever so slightly. I have never observed rain or any other recognizable weather feature, but I believe there is a faint wind, too weak to register on my instruments.

Yates closed the last of the journals that he had brought up to the library. He was trying to decide whether to fetch a new batch when he heard the front doors rattle and open. The sound took him by surprise and he jumped up from his seat, but then a familiar voice called out.

"Mr. Yates? Are you there?" It was Cabot, the caretaker.

Cabot apologized for not looking in on him sooner. "Some damn bug got me. I've been in bed ever since the night you arrived. My wife wouldn't let me out of bed and I had to wait until she'd gone shopping to sneak out."

They were sitting in the kitchen drinking soda, the only thing Yates had available to offer.

"You still look a little pale."

"The wife'll fix me up if she doesn't kill me first. How've you been getting along? Did the cleaning people come by?"

"Yes, they did. I've made progress." Yates thought about the basement and decided it was too early to mention it to Cabot. In fact, it might be best to inform Arthur Winslow first and let him decide what to do about it. "A little slower than I expected, but it's coming along." Actually he'd been ahead of schedule until he had found the basement entrance.

"No spooks or anything?"

"No. Why do you ask? Is this place supposed to be haunted by Emma Winslow or something?"

Cabot shook his head. "Not really. She didn't die here anyway. They'd taken her to a nursing home before the end. I've been in and out of the place for a couple of months now and I've never seen anything amiss. But I have to tell you that once or twice I thought someone was watching, particularly in there." He nodded in the direction of the library. "I'm not a superstitious man, but sometimes a place just doesn't feel right."

Yates glanced around. "It's not the most cheerful place."

Cabot drained his can of soda and set it down. "Well, I just wanted you to know I hadn't forgotten about you." And a few minutes later he was gone.

It had turned dark outside and Yates decided the rest of the journals could wait until the following day.

Yates felt an odd reluctance to descend into the basement the following morning. He called in an order for groceries to a local market that offered a delivery service and took a brief walk on the grounds before entering the library. There he booted up his laptops and settled back into the rhythm of cataloguing and valuing books. He managed to immerse himself in the familiar task and continued, making good progress, until a knock on the door brought him out to accept delivery of his order. Then, of course, he had to put it away and his stomach rumbled a bit so he had lunch. But when that was over and he returned to the library, his thoughts kept straying to the pile of journals he had read the previous day. Finally, he picked them up, opened the hatch, and brought them down to the basement.

Nothing looked any different except that the hoe he had leaned against the back of the staircase was now lying flat on the floor. He assumed it had fallen over during the night. After swapping what he carried for the years 1970 through 1980, almost more than he could safely carry, he glanced around one last time before mounting the stairs. The feeling of being watched was almost imperceptible now and he dismissed it as an echo of his earlier over reaction rather than a new response.

The first five years were so routine and uninformative than Yates almost went back to his real work. Mrs. Gibson, cook and housekeeper, was hired in 1975. During the course of 1976, Winslow built a new viewing screen, based on an original concept which he maddeningly did not describe except to call it the Meniscus.

Since the Meniscus is more akin to a motion picture projection than a television screen, I am able to generate a much larger image, limited only by my physical surroundings. More importantly, there is no loss of definition so I am able to examine details much more closely. Faint movement is now quite visible and I can report here that there is a nearly constant wind, or more properly a breeze, in the viewed area. I have also detected very faint details in the distance including motion in a direction contrary to that of the wind, which always blows left to right from my viewpoint. These sightings are infrequent and I have been unable to ascertain any detail. It is likely that there are eddies in the wind pattern based on the configuration of the ground. I continue to be frustrated in my attempts to expand the scene or pan in any direction.

Winslow spent two full years redesigning and rebuilding the Interpreter. Fortunately he provided a series of sketches and Yates was confident that at least externally it matched the machine in the basement. There were also diagrams showing the various controls, but the labels were no more informative than those on the machine itself. Winslow was unable to view the desert scene for almost eight months while he was rebuilding the Interpreter, but when he renewed his observations he reported only superficial changes that were "probably the result of mild erosion."

He also mentioned a problem that had apparently existed all along but which he had never previously recorded. In order to document his discovery, Winslow had taken photographs with a variety of cameras and types of film. All of these had shown a blank space, featureless, uninformative. A motion picture camera had fared no better. No effort had been made, as far as could be gleaned from the journals, to bring in an outside witness, although Winslow mentioned having communicated his success to at least three of his correspondents, two in Europe and one in Japan.

The entries during the late 1970s were much longer but much more technical and Yates did a good deal of skimming. Winslow continued to refine the Interpreter but had not solved any of his basic problems. He could not change the view, nor could he record it any form. But in 1980 there were two significant events.

The first was his sighting of a very large shape in the distance. He had nothing by which to register scale, but he sensed that the dimly seen form that appeared in the periphery of his viewing field was gigantic, "like a skyscraper mounted on wheels." Winslow had not speculated about its nature but noted that it moved steadily until it passed behind an irregularity that he believed to be a chain of mountains. They might, of course, have been the size of divots.

Winslow's second discovery was more significant. The view had always been merely a projection according to the notes, although it was "comprised of the loci of realized potentials", whatever that might be. There was nothing resembling a conventional movie projector in the diagrams. Nevertheless, it had functioned that way. A hand or other object passed through the image without any sensation, distorting it slightly as would happen with a motion picture if something passed in front of the lens, returning to its original state when that object was removed.

During one period of observation, Winslow had been crouched in front of the image trying to see some small feature more clearly when he had lost his balance. Instinctively he raised a hand to catch hold of something. As always, it passed through the image but this time he felt something, a very mild resistance that lasted only a fraction of a second. He withdrew his hand, then extended it again. The sensation repeated itself. There was some physical component now, perhaps some sort of localized energy, or at least so he had speculated.

Predictably, this became the focus of Winslow's subsequent research.

Yates made one more trip down to the basement and brought up another stack of journals. The feeling that he was not alone returned, however, so he took the first three, tucked them under an arm, closed the doors, and went up to his bedroom.

It was tedious reading and his interest flagged more than once. Yates was good at his job because once he started a project, he became determined to finish it, and finish it with the same degree of care as when it was started. Having decided to read Otis Winslow's journals in their entirety, he was psychologically incapable of abandoning the endeavor. He plodded on through technical descriptions he could not decipher and theoretical ones that he barely understood.

Eventually a growing suspicion was confirmed by a single short paragraph.

I am certain now that what the Interpreter generates is not a window but a door. A storm door might be a better term since it is possible to see what is on the other side through an invisible barrier. Professor Kalish has suggested that with a more robust power source I might be able to punch a way through, but I have my doubts. I have varied the power level already and there is no measurable effect on the interface. I am more inclined to think that there are erroneous assumptions in the calculations which have allowed me to approximate rather than reach a solution. There have been certain contradictory assumptions which I have tried to reconcile but perhaps by doing so I have adulterated the purity of

*the equations upon which my work is based. I shall have to develop
alternate strategies using different configurations. It might take
years to find the right template, but I have nothing left but years.*

Yates was still wide awake so he retrieved the rest of the
journals from the library. Winslow grew increasingly discouraged
during 1982 and the entries were terse and uninformative. Then, in
February of 1983, something happened that he hadn't expected.
Something was looking through from the other side.

*It must have arrived sometime during the night, although I
don't understand how it was able to determine the location of the
Meniscus, since the Interpreter was turned off as usual while I was
not present. But as soon as the image appeared this morning, it was
standing there – if that's the right term – motionless. It had no eyes,
or at least nothing that I recognized as such, but there was no doubt
in my mind that it was able to perceive the Meniscus and possibly
even look into our world. More than ever I regret being unable to
take photographs because any description I might write down will be
totally inadequate. My first impression was of a starfish tilted
upright, although the number of limbs does not seem to be constant.
Possibly they emerge from and withdraw into the central mass,
although I have never witnessed either process. Their number just
appears to vary spontaneously.*

*The surface is probably viscous although there are areas
which might be covered with fur, or perhaps very fine cilia. I cannot
be certain which, if either. The central mass includes features which
are literally painful to look at. I cannot yet be more precise.
Although I lack any way of evaluating its size, I believe it to be
somewhat larger than a man, particularly in breadth. Its body
obscures most of the familiar view but what I can see of it seems to
be otherwise unchanged.*

The situation also remained unchanged for the next few days.
Winslow was excited and intensely curious but did not seem
remotely worried, not even when something unexpected occurred.

*My counterpart – as I think of the creature who stares
unblinkingly into my basement – is no longer alone. To his left – my*

right – I can see another very similar creature in the distance. I observed this second individual throughout the morning and it is just discernibly closer. Either it moves with painful slowness or time does not function in the same manner as in our world. Nor am I able to determine its method of locomotion.

Perhaps unwisely, I approached the Meniscus and touched it with the tip of one finger. Its elasticity may have increased slightly but it still resists any attempt to penetrate it. The first creature showed no visible reaction to my effort but I am confident that it is aware of my presence. I have found a reference in the Necronomicon to "scavengers of the gods," who were "like unto the stars themselves and possessors of the patience of eternity." I wonder if this refers to my new acquaintances.

The secondary figure disappeared somewhere out of the field of view, but it took seven months to cover the distance. The situation remained otherwise unchanged until the fall of 1986, at which point Winslow had implemented some "radically altered protocols". He reported an improvement in focus but lamented that the revisions had also resulted in "uncontrollable fluctuations" that resembled ripples passing through the Meniscus. And then came November 1.

I have been rather disappointed that the recent adjustments have had no noticeable impact on the stability of the image. I confess that I grew rather upset and terminated today's session much earlier than usual rather than watch the continued disruptions in the Meniscus. I stood staring blankly for a good length of time, unable to think of a new approach, and it was only by chance that I noticed a sprinkling of very light, very pale sand on the floor beneath the now featureless wall. There had been a comparatively stiff breeze in that other realm and it appears that it had blown these particles through the Meniscus.

It seemed too good to be true. I was concerned that I might have tracked something in myself, so I initiated a new session. The scene was unchanged and the fluctuations continued. I thought twice about touching it with my finger this time and selected a pencil from my desk instead. Alas, although I could distinctly feel the surface yield slightly, it soon became as rigid as ever. Thoughtfully, I gathered up all of the sand I could find – it barely covered the palm of one hand – and tossed it lightly at the bottom of the image, not wanting my counterpart to interpret it as a hostile act.

Most of it rebounded, but at least a portion passed through. The doorway is there but I still don't understand how it can be permeable at one point and not at another.

Winslow wrestled with the problem into early 1987 before calling a sudden temporary halt to his experiments. A correspondent identified only as TNP had urged him to consult the works of one Ludwig Prinn. Winslow had done so and whatever he read there alarmed him.

I have allowed my desire to satisfy my curiosity to overrun my sense of caution. As TNP suggested, Prinn's "gatherers" correspond to the scavengers referred to in the Necronomicon, and his wariness is understandable. They are likely also what Harada referred to as the "patient devourers" and the "hungry ones" alluded to in Vulrich. So even though I am confident that I know now how to eliminate the membrane between realities, I will not attempt to implement my latest revision until I have taken certain precautions. To do otherwise would be unconscionable given the consequences if one of these creatures should be allowed to pass through the Meniscus.

This was the point at which Winslow began planning the modifications to the basement. He first had a new wall poured to bifurcate the space. The older, conventional staircase was removed and the spiral one installed "with an opening small enough that no unwelcome guest would be able to pass through." Winslow also talked about the "ikiryo" without explaining its nature. Apparently it referred to a kind of astral projection and he believed that it was something the scavengers – as he now referred to the star shaped creatures – could generate as an act of will. "I am afraid they may have already examined the basement in this manner, which means that nothing I contrive will bar their further entry, although their physical bodies may still be constrained. They may yet be able to cause physical manifestations even in a non-corporal state, but they are thankfully sluggish even in their ethereal forms."

There was a brief mention of the installation of the "faceplate", which Yates assumed was the hatchway to the staircase. Then came a surprising entry in early June.

I have approved the plans for the alterations in the library. Hale clearly thinks I'm deranged but he won't turn down such a profitable job. I had originally planned to install the casters under the entire floor, but he estimates that would take more than a year to implement, if it is possible at all. I have compromised on the four interlocking sections that I had originally planned and must be content with that. As it is, this will not be completed before the end of the year.

The mechanism will be as simple and maintenance free as I can make it. The master control will activate it at midnight on every second day so long as there is an ample electric supply. The four sections will allow only about two dozen possible combinations, but the scavengers are known for their persistence not their intelligence. The ikiryo would take weeks or even months to find its way out of the library even if the configuration was static. A change every second day will be more than sufficient to keep it confused, forced to unlearn what it has already experienced, and by the time it has recouped its loss, the maze of shelves will have been altered yet again.

Winslow went into more detail during the next few months but the gist of it was that there were devices beneath the library floor that moved one or more units of shelving into a new position every forty-eight hours. No wonder Yates had been disoriented. And that must be the grating sound that he had heard at night.

Yates retrieved the rest of the journals – it took two trips – and began to read obsessively. Winslow had noticed that the original scavenger was now gradually moving out of view to the left. He was ready to launch a new effort to penetrate the interface but had been reluctant to do so while it was, so to speak, staring him in the face. His impatience got the better of him, however, and he implemented it while a significant portion of the creature remained on screen. And he succeeded this time.

There was only the faintest resistance before my probe passed completely through the Meniscus and I actually drew a circle in the sand of another world. There was no discernible reaction by the scavenger, but its reactions are so slow that it could be terrified, puzzled, or enraged and I would not be able to tell. I used a ladle to scoop up enough sand to fill a gallon jug and in the process uncovered something that did not appear to be a rock. I retrieved a set of tongs from the kitchen and pulled it loose and then through the Meniscus. It resembles a fallen branch although of no species I recognize and it is possibly not even organic. There is nothing else within my reach at present. Tomorrow I will bring in some of the garden tools and try again.

Winslow expressed his frustration frequently in the months that followed. He was still unable to change the view in any fashion, which limited his ability to gather samples. On impulse one day he rashly reached through the Meniscus with his arm but withdrew it quickly. "I have never felt such biting cold." He used the tongs to deposit odd items onto the other worldly sands – a flower, a bottle of wine, a trowel. The flower wilted in minutes, disintegrated and blew away. The bottle exploded. The trowel lay inert and was slowly covered by drifting sand.

Yates thought he detected contradictory feelings in the journals for 1989 and 1990. On the one hand, Winslow was elated by his discoveries and accomplishments and eager to learn more. Although he was secretive about his work – only a few correspondents were privy to any real information and none of them knew the whole story – he hoped someday to make them public. On the other hand, he began to worry that he had moved too far too quickly. There was no question that he was meddling with the unknown and with no knowledge of the consequences. He had also somewhat tardily paid attention to the warnings that were appended to the source material he had consulted.

Winslow's entries became even more guarded in 1991 when the scavenger returned, a process that took months before it was in full view. There was no way to tell if it was the same one, but that probably didn't matter. It was clear that the creature was aware of Winslow, or at least of the Meniscus, and curious about it. And one day an appendage that moved so slowly that its motion was invisible to the eye began to come closer and closer and Winslow realized that the scavenger was going to try to pierce the barrier from the other side. In a panic, he turned off the Interpreter and fled upstairs "shaken to the core of my being."

He didn't venture back to the hidden room for almost a week and even then he had to force himself down the staircase. Although he could not explain why he felt such sudden, deep rooted dread, it was nevertheless real.

Upon returning, all seemed unchanged. He had turned off the Interpreter so the Meniscus was not visible. But he did notice an oddity on the wall where it normally manifested itself. There was a very faint bulge which puzzled him somewhat until he realized its significance. It was the outer surface of one of the scavenger's appendages. It had never occurred to Winslow to wonder what would happen if the Meniscus closed while he was extending some object through it. Would it be cleanly severed with a portion in each reality? That seemed the most likely outcome and even though he was filled with revulsion, he was also entranced with the possibility of studying this fragment at close hand.

He had recorded its measurements in his journal and outlined a series of tests he planned to perform, but in fact he probably never reached that point. Suffering from nervous exhaustion, he had gone to bed and slept heavily until morning. After eating the breakfast that Mrs. Gordon laid out for him, he descended in somewhat better spirits that lasted only until he decided to double check his observations from the previous day. To his astonishment and growing horror, he discovered that the fragment was now slightly larger. He had no choice but to conclude that somehow the Meniscus remained open, perhaps because of some unknowable mechanism on the other side, perhaps simply because he had weakened the barrier between universes in some fashion

Winslow tried to reassure himself that the Meniscus was too small to allow the scavenger to pass through, but that presupposed that it must remain upright. He had never seen the creature in any other posture, but that didn't mean that it wasn't possible for it to incline itself forward and half crawl into the hidden room.

Attempts were made to repel the scavenger's advance. Winslow attacked the intrusion with a hammer and chisel, a blow torch, a variety of acids and other chemicals. There was no discernible effect in any of these cases. He was afraid to turn the Interpreter on because he feared that might make the situation worse. He considered contacting the authorities but decided against it, in part because of his ingrained habit of secrecy, in part because he feared that they would underestimate the danger and refuse to allow any further attempt to bar the advance of what they might interpret as an emissary from another world. If they believed him in the first place.

After several weeks, more than twelve inches of the appendage had emerged. It seemed darker than when perceived through the Meniscus, and was slightly flexible despite its impenetrable surface. Winslow had written to a number of correspondents, most of whom were apparently convinced that he had become delusional. Yates found himself increasingly sympathetic to that view. A few made suggestions which Winslow attempted to implement. None of them had any effect.

When a second appendage began to appear, Winslow panicked. He removed certain components from the Interpreter to render it inoperable and carried them up to the library. There was no mention of their eventual fate. July 1, 1991 was the very last time he entered the hidden room, or at least the last mentioned in any of the journals, which Yates finished reading in a state of mingled horror and disbelief.

An entry in 1993 was particularly unsettling.

I can hear it moving beneath the floor now. My estimate of the time it would require to pass completely through the interface was quite accurate. I imagine that it is examining the Interpreter although I don't know what its alien intelligence will make of the mechanism. It is in any case of no use without the elements which I have disposed of. Although I am reasonably confident that it cannot physically escape except back through the interface into its own world, I fear that Von Bek and Mikushima were correct. There was a definite presence in the library this evening and it can only be that the scavenger has let loose its ikiryo to explore where it cannot physically enter. I can only pray that my preparations were well conceived and that they can contain it.

And a few weeks later.

There is no question now that I am not alone. Although all is silent beneath the floor, that is not the case in the library. Books fall off their shelves with no visible agency involved. The ikiryo's ability to affect the material world is fortunately extremely limited. I visit the library on a daily basis to reassure myself that the stalemate still holds. My hope is that my visitor will realize that further progress is impossible and withdraw through the Meniscus but I recognize that there is so much disparity in the perception of time between the two of us that I might be long dead before then. I can only do what I can do and hope for the best.

From that point on the journals consisted of short, infrequent, and repetitive paragraphs. Winslow gradually abandoned his correspondence and apparently gave up his research as well, settling into the role of reclusive guardian. What he proposed to do in the event that his safeguards failed was less clear. In 1998 one of the floor mechanisms jammed. Fortunately Winslow had insisted that they be accessible for maintenance from above, because he hadn't wanted anyone to know about the basement room. It was successfully repaired within the week.

Yates set down the journal for 2014. Winslow had not mentioned any presentiment that his health was failing. It may well have taken him by surprise. His story – imaginary or otherwise – had stayed consistent until the end. Despite his own unsettling experiences, Yates was inclined to believe that Winslow had been delusional. There was certainly no lurking presence in the basement now, and there were likely perfectly mundane explanations for the rest. The faint rumbling from downstairs – the library was in motion once again – caused him to glance at his watch. It was midnight. Crazy or not, Winslow had designed his safeguards to last. Yates leaned back against the pillows and almost immediately fell asleep.

Yates felt a great sense of well being in the morning. He made himself a larger than usual breakfast and ate it with relish. Finishing the last of the journals had cleared his mental desk of a distraction and he now felt an increased determination to get back to the job for which he had been hired. With luck his preliminary survey would take only a few more days and he would have a comprehensive proposal for the disposition of the books and papers to present to Arthur Winslow. His grandfather had undoubtedly been a brilliant, though deeply disturbed man, whose illusions were no doubt aggravated by his isolated circumstances. Yates recognized that even he had been affected by the atmosphere of the place. But he was determined on a more pragmatic and sensible course of action now.

The books from the basement were just books, though valuable ones. The *Necronomicon* would have to be returned to its rightful owner, but the others were a legitimate part of the estate insofar as he could determine. He decided to make one final trip to the basement to gather them up and add them to the small pile of volumes which he felt should be sold off individually. It would be the last time he would need to descend into the basement. The hidden room would be Arthur Winslow's problem now.

Despite his conviction that Winslow had been suffering from dementia, Yates could not avoid feeling a faint trepidation as he descended into the basement and he found himself glancing around warily almost without realizing what he was doing. Then he shook himself, mentally if not physically, and went over to the shelves, carefully taking down the volumes he had deemed valuable. He had thought about returning the journals from his bedroom, but they would all have to be brought upstairs eventually in any case so he'd left them where they were.

Conscious that this might be his last visit, he walked over to the machine, wondering if it had ever functioned at all. He was ready, even eager, to dismiss Winslow's account entirely now, although he was never tempted to try what he believed was the main power switch. It might explode or short out and cause a fire, after all. Then he moved to the far wall, where the loops of cabling still outlined an immense oval. This, presumably, was the Meniscus, the focal point for Winslow's visual illusions. Impulsively he took a coin from his pocket and tossed it directly at the plastered wall.

The coin disappeared.

Yates stood there dumbfounded, then gradually became aware of a change. The air was stirring, a definite breeze where no breeze should have existed. And it was cold, so cold that he shivered, or maybe that wasn't really why he shivered.

Because the Meniscus opened and Yates was no longer alone.

THE NEW GUY

The new guy was a little bit weird. Chloe had checked him out right away, carrying some paperwork to the mail room that could have waited until after lunch, just so she had an excuse to walk past his cubicle. It was only a quick look, of course, and you couldn't tell anything about personality or even personal hygiene. He was tallish and a trifle thin, she thought, and his skin was so pale that she wondered if he'd been sick. He was facing his terminal, running through the tutorial, so she only saw a portion of his profile. Her preliminary opinion was that he was nothing special but potentially of interest.

It was at lunch that she learned his name. She had made a point of sitting with Marcia Clark in the cafeteria because Marcia worked in personnel and would probably have handled his paperwork. The new guy had brought his own food in a featureless black lunchbox and was sitting by himself in one corner. He had very dark hair which fell over his forehead like a curtain and he kept his head down, concentrating on a sandwich.

"So who's the new guy?" Chloe asked with just the right degree of indifference.

Marcia followed her eyes. "Oh, him. His name's Duane Hadley. Twenty-four years old, no living relatives, lives out west of town. He comes to us from Eblis Manufacturing. Staff reductions. Boilerplate recommendation. I thought he was kind of creepy but that's just me." Marcia found something wrong with everyone they hired.

"Married?"

"Nope. I think he might be gay." Any new hire who didn't come on to her was probably gay as far as Marcia was concerned.

"He's kind of cute in a whipped puppy sort of way."

Marcia gave a theatrical sigh. "This isn't going to be another one of your projects, is it?"

"I don't know. I'm thinking about it. It looks like he could use a friend."

Marcia reached across the table and touched Chloe's forearm. "One of these days you're going to get yourself into trouble, you know. Sometimes people are just fine and don't need or want outside help. Remember what happened with Albert."

"His name was Alfred and that wasn't my fault. How was I supposed to know that he was a racist asshole?"

"You might have checked around before arranging a blind date with Naomi. I still think that's why she quit."

Chloe shook her head. "Alfred was gone by then. He was fired, remember?"

"Yeah, but everyone here knew about the fight and she was obviously still uncomfortable."

"Well, I'll be more careful this time."

Chloe didn't actually speak to Duane until the following day when she stopped by his cubicle to introduce herself. "So how are you adjusting to Sheffield Data Services?"

Duane had a gravelly voice that was so low it was almost inaudible and his eyes kept moving around the room, never meeting hers. His hands – the fingers seemed unusually long and slender – were clamped together in his lap, having retreated from the keyboard as soon as she attracted his attention. "It's all right. I'll be fine once I get up to speed on the systems here."

"My cubicle is the last on the right, so if you need anything, just let me know."

"Thanks, but I think I'm okay." He turned back to the monitor, dismissing her.

Chloe was neither discouraged nor affronted. Duane was obviously an introvert, uneasy with strangers. She would just have to arrange things so that she was no longer a stranger.

But she wouldn't just rush into things without developing some background first. Her experience with Alfred Sloan had taught her the risks of mixing unknown elements and taking things for granted. Things had gotten out of control and Chloe was always unhappy when she wasn't in control of a situation. That's why she spent so much time practicing her martial arts. You never knew when some asshole would think he was going to call the shots just because he was bigger than she was. If she was going to do something to improve the quality of Duane's life – she always characterized her projects as being for the benefit of others – then she had to understand just what it was that he was lacking.

She knew better than to ask Marcia for Duane's home address, but she had let drop that he lived somewhere on the west side of Managansett, an area mostly heavily wooded except for the low income housing project, which was probably where Duane lived. Chloe checked the phone book but he was either unlisted or only had a cell phone, probably the latter. She also tried googling him, but there were so many Duane Hadleys that she gave up and when she added the town name she only got blends of Duane somebody and somebody else Hadley.

But Chloe always enjoyed a challenge, except of course the challenge of her own life. She was twenty-five years old, reasonably attractive, had a good job and a nice apartment. She considered herself successful, popular, and possessed of a bright future. Except that she had no vision of what that future might be, and no friends except casual acquaintances at work who never socialized with her elsewhere, and her job was routine and boring with no obvious path to promotion, and her apartment was neat and clean but in a declining neighborhood. Even her cats had run away – three of them in two years. Her parents had moved to Oregon – they answered her emails occasionally. She had no other relatives except a great aunt in a nursing home whom she never visited, and the aunt had Alzheimer's in any case. Her last date had been during her senior year of high school and she was still a virgin.

The following day she tried to follow Duane home from work. He had a rather old Honda with visible rust, but she wasn't quick enough and lost him before they were out of the parking lot. The day after that she made sure that she was out of the building before him, and she maneuvered so she was right behind his car as they passed the security shack.

They went west on Main Street and Chloe nodded to herself, confident that she was right about where he lived, but he drove past the entrance and turned right on Reservoir Road. There weren't many houses up that way and only about half of the farms were still operating. She supposed he might not be going directly home – this route eventually led to the next town, Scituate – but she stayed behind him anyway, dropping back a bit so that hopefully he wouldn't notice her.

When he finally turned off, she almost missed him because the driveway was narrow and overgrown. There was a sign on a tree that read HADLEY FARM just above a battered mailbox, but the sign was so old and worn that it was barely legible. Chloe drove past and found a place where she could pull off the road and park, then took her cell phone out and walked back to take two quick pictures, one of the driveway and the other of the sign.

The farm was obviously not in production and had not been for some time. The fields that she could see had gone wild and the house was barely visible from the roadway. She walked back and forth and took a couple more pictures, but she knew they wouldn't be satisfactory, and in any case the light was fading. Feeling mildly disappointed but not discouraged, she returned to her car and drove home.

Chloe's apartment was actually a retrofit of an old motel that had gone out of business. It consisted of two of the original units, inexpertly merged into a single area, with a tiny kitchenette replacing the second bathroom. This left two other rooms, one in which she slept, the other divided by a folding screen into a kind of sitting room in front and what she thought of as her office in the rear. She popped a frozen dinner into the microwave and went to the office, connecting her cell phone to the still booting PC so that she could upload the pictures and print out copies of those worth keeping. A wooden shelving unit beside her desk held a dozen scrapbooks, the records of her previous projects. They bore labels reading Alfred Sloan, Naomi Becker, Paul Bernstein, Alicia Cramer, and others. Some of them bulged with photographs and commentary, some were quite slender. Chloe kept electronic copies of everything, of course, but she much preferred to leaf through physical evidence of her work.

A new book, labeled Duane Hadley but empty so far except for one furtively snapped picture she had taken at work, lay on the desk. Chloe brought up her latest photos, sent two of them to the printer, then went back to check on her supper and take a cold beer from the tiny refrigerator. She ate her Thai sesame noodles while staring at the three photographs. It seemed that Duane might present some early challenges, but that was just as well. It wouldn't be as satisfying if it was too easy.

Chloe began watching for excuses to talk to Duane on the job, but he had apparently picked up the necessary skills fairly easily and was already being given regular assignments. He had declined any assistance on the three occasions when she had offered it, once with a slightly testy tone that irritated her. She was only trying to help, after all. Why was it that so many people seemed to resent her good intentions? On two occasions she had invited herself to sit at his table in the cafeteria, but he had been reading an old hardcover book both times and had not responded to her overtures with anything other than monosyllables. Chloe had trained herself to smoke so that she could join the group who went out to the rear parking lot to indulge themselves, but apparently Duane hadn't picked up the habit.

The weekend came but that helped rather than hindered her campaign. Chloe parked in the parking lot for the Loft – the town's only night spot had closed down last year and seemed unlikely to reopen any time soon, donned her small back pack, and set off into the woods. She wasn't entirely sure where the state watershed land ended and the private property began, but she figured if it wasn't posted it was fair game.

It took almost an hour before she sighted the Hadley house. The barn was long gone but most of the stone fences were intact and that was the only way she could trace the outlines of what had formerly been fields. She worked her way around the perimeter and found a better line of sight to the house. There was a good sized vegetable garden behind it, far enough away to be out of the building's shadow. There was also an old well, a tractor so caked with rust that it had lost most of its surface features, a small henhouse with a collapsed roof, and a windowless wooden shed about the size of a two car garage. There was no sign of life and she couldn't see the driveway, so had no way of determining whether or not Duane was at home. She took a few pictures and moved on.

On the opposite side of the house she ventured onto the property directly, sheltered from view by a handful of apple trees. She worked her way carefully, trying to stay out of sight without looking as though she was trying to stay out of sight. If discovered, she had her cover story. She wanted to lose a little weight so she had decided to take up hiking, something she could do cheaply and on her own. She would be ever so apologetic to learn that she had strayed onto private property. But so far she hadn't seen a soul.

Chloe came quite close to the house, closer than she had planned. She stopped then and saw Duane's car parked on the gravel driveway. It was too soon to make a direct approach and she was about to turn away when a screen door slammed. She crouched instinctively, but Duane went directly to his car. It took a couple of tries before the engine caught and then he was turning around and headed back toward the road.

The timing could not have been better.

Although Marcia had indicated that Duane had no living relatives, she still proceeded cautiously. Once past the end of the old orchard, she took a picture of the house. From this close she could see that it was in bad shape. The paint was peeling enthusiastically, there were cracks in two of the windows on this side, and a few shingles were missing from the roof. There was a small half porch on the front, but some of the spindles were missing. The shades were drawn on all of the windows.

There was a dented aluminum trashcan. Chloe lifted the lid and peered inside, wrinkling her nose at the rancid smell. Right on top was a full color catalog with a mailing label addressed to Duane Hadley. Using just the tips of two fingers, she lifted it out and dropped it to the ground, flipping it over with her foot so that she could see the front. It was from something called The Grotto and the legend read "Supplies for collectors and practitioners of the occult." The cover was decorated with a grinning skull that sported a lighted candle growing out of its top.

Chloe crouched and tentatively turned a few pages. There were a lot of herbs and other bottled and boxed items deriving from plants and animals, a good deal of jewelry, an entire page of colored feathers, some pottery including mortars and pestles, two pages of books – some of which were priced well over a hundred dollars, a variety of hand tools whose purpose she could not decipher, and even some highly decorative clothing.

She took a picture of the cover and then carefully dropped the catalog back in with the garbage and closed the lid. So Duane was into witchcraft of some sort. That had possibilities.

The porch offered nothing of interest. The cane backed rocking chair had a broken runner and there were loose boards. The curtain at one of the front windows wasn't quite closed and she tried to peer through. The interior was so dark that she couldn't see anything, although for a second she thought something had moved across her field of view. She considered trying the door but decided against it. Maybe another time.

The yard on the opposite side was better kept, although the rusting tractor loomed over it like an angel of neglect. The shed seemed to be relatively new and the padlock on the door was locked and shiny. There was some kind of machinery running inside, she decided, because she could hear a faint but rhythmic rushing sound, almost like breathing. Not a generator, she decided, or a conventional motor. More like a compressor. Chloe took more pictures, then walked out to the road and back to her car. It was a good start.

A trip to the town hall during her lunch hour confirmed that the property in question – it encompassed about thirty acres – was owned by one Duane Hadley, who had succeeded Oliver and Dorothy Hadley in the title registry. The bored clerk who provided a copy of the document in question could tell her nothing additional. Back home she took to the internet again and discovered that Oliver and Dorothy had both perished when their barn burned to the ground four years earlier. Duane was mentioned in passing as their only child.

Two more attempts to open a conversation with Duane were rebuffed, or perhaps more accurately fell unacknowledged. Duane had never been observed speaking to anyone except in the line of work as far as Chloe could determine. Some of the other employees were already referring to him as "odd" or even "spooky", but his work was accurate and more than adequate.

The following Saturday, Chloe visited the offices of the *Managansett Monitor*, a weekly that was mostly advertisements since its last change of ownership although it had formerly been rather more newsy. An elderly woman somewhat reluctantly admitted that they kept back issues and that Chloe could look through them. She found the story about the fire, but it was only two paragraphs long. The town's fire chief thought lightning had hit the barn, that the Hadleys had gone out to try to deal with the fire themselves - they had no telephone – and that they'd been overcome by the smoke. Their son Duane had rushed back from Maine, where he'd been visiting friends. The friends were not named.

Chloe took a picture of the news story for her scrapbook.

"So how's the project coming?" Marcia asked at lunch the following Monday.

Chloe stiffened a little. Marcia was teasing, but it was closer to the truth than she realized. "What do you mean?"

"I thought you were going to help the new guy out of his shell."

"Oh, you mean Duane. I'd almost forgotten about him. You know I only help out when I'm wanted, Marcia."

"Yeah, right."

Chloe thought that she had been right not to take on Marcia as a project. She didn't deserve the honor.

Duane had his book again at lunch that day. Chloe managed to drop her bag as she walked by and, as she crouched to retrieve it, managed to read the title. It was in German. *Unaussprechlichen Kulten.* Chloe's grandparents had escaped from East Germany during the 1970s and never learned much English. Chloe was quite fluent. She carefully committed the title to memory until she was out of the cafeteria, then jotted it down in a notebook.

Chloe was convinced she was beginning to understand Duane now. He was obviously smart and intellectually inclined, but hopelessly shy. His interest in the occult – more convincing than ever when she looked up the strange book title that evening and discovered that it was a rare book dealing with some obscure religion – was probably part of his quest to find a group to which he could attach himself. He was an only child and his home was so physically isolated that he must have had few if any playmates. She would not be surprised to discover that he had been home schooled. She didn't remember him from high school and they were about the same age. In her judgment he was crying out for companionship, but so inexperienced that he was frightened to take concrete steps in that direction for fear of rejection.

Chloe had read a good deal of pop psychology.

It seemed obvious to her that if left to himself, Duane would remain trapped by his own reticence indefinitely. Friday afternoon she set about organizing one of the occasional but irregular after work expeditions to the bar at the Managansett Inn. There the rank and file at the office could grouse about work with little fear of being overheard and subsequent repercussions. Several people turned her down but there were others who welcomed the excuse and once she had them lined up, she walked over to Duane's cubicle.

"If you don't have any plans this evening, some of us are going out for a drink and I wondered if you'd like to come along."

Duane looked at her as though she had addressed him in a foreign language. "Why would I want to do that?"

The question was so baldly stated that it disconcerted her. "Well, it will give you a chance to meet some people. Make friends. You know."

Duane seemed to be giving the subject some deep thought. "I don't think so," he answered at last. "I don't think anyone here would be interested in me, and I'm not interested in any of them."

Chloe didn't have a prepared response to that one. "Some other time then," she offered vaguely and went back to her own cubicle.

Chloe felt stymied and she didn't like that at all. In all of her previous projects, she had developed multiple lines of approach, gathered considerable data ahead of time, and although the outcome had not always been – in fact had rarely been – what she had desired, she was always able to dismiss her failures as shortcomings of her subject, not a fault in her planning. But Duane was a bit of an enigma. He seemed to have no life outside of work. She had driven by his house several times and repeated her hiking reconnaissance twice, but she hadn't learned anything significant. On one occasion she had watched from hiding as he unlocked the shed and went inside, but he had closed the doors behind him and she had gotten bored and left before he reappeared.

She followed him home from work a couple of times, but the only stop he had ever made had been at the grocery mart downtown. One Saturday she spotted the UPS truck coming out of Duane's driveway, but no other vehicle had ventured inside except, presumably, the mail truck. At least not while she was watching. And she spent an increasing amount of time clandestinely observing the farmhouse, partly because she didn't like being frustrated, partly because she had no other active projects going an it was very important to her that she have a purpose. Chloe needed to be wanted, even if those who wanted her remained unaware of their need for her help.

Nevertheless, she was growing increasingly discouraged by late autumn. She and Duane had exchanged less than fifty words during the previous four weeks, all of them work related. He didn't seem to bear her any ill will; he was merely indifferent. Their mutual boss publicly praised him for his productivity. He was indifferent to that as well.

So it came as a complete surprise when he knocked on the side of her cubicle one day.

"Hi, Duane. What can I do for you?"

"I think I was a little bit rude to you a while ago. I wanted to apologize." He smiled, but the expression looked uncomfortable on his face.

Chloe brightened a bit. Maybe he wasn't a lost cause after all. "That's all right. Water under the bridge and all that."

"No, I really want to make it up to you. I wondered if you had any plans for Saturday."

This was not a scenario that she had considered. Chloe saw herself as the master planner who moved other people around, for their own good of course. She had never dated any of her projects. On the other hand, she had made no progress in learning more about the real Duane Hadley which she believed hovered somewhere hidden from view and this might be the best, the only way in which she could penetrate his reserve.

"Nothing I can't break. Why?"

"Well, I have some friends coming over to my place for the weekend. We're going to have a cookout and stuff. I thought, if you weren't doing anything that is, that you might want to come along."

Chloe knew she shouldn't seem too eager. "I don't know. They'd all be strangers. Maybe they wouldn't like me."

His smile suddenly seemed more genuine. "Oh, they'll like you just fine. Trust me on that."

She pretended to be undecided, then nodded. "All right then. I'll be there." She remembered then that she wasn't supposed to know where he lived. "But I'll need directions."

Duane handed her a slip of paper. "I wrote them down. Things will start around three in the afternoon. And I have something planned for later on that will really impress you."

"Thanks."

Duane turned and went back to his cubicle.

Chloe spent a considerable amount of time deciding what to wear on Saturday. It was an outdoorsy type of thing so she needed to dress casual, but not too casual. She settled on her best pair of jeans and a plain but nice blouse. She timed things so that she arrived a few minutes after three. Duane's car was parked in front of the house and there was a black van with Maine license plates next to it. She pulled over so that she wasn't blocking anyone in and was not even out of the car when Duane showed up. He was even smiling.

"I was afraid you weren't going to make it."

"I just mislaid my car keys. They fell down behind the radiator and it took forever to find them."

"Come meet the others."

He led her around the side of the house. A long table had been set up in front of the shed and a charcoal grill was smoking alongside. She saw chips, potato salad, uncooked hamburgers and hotdogs, and the associated rolls and condiments. The plates were paper and the utensils plastic.

There were two people standing nearby. One was a cadaverously tall man with shoulder length hair, a scruffy beard, and tattoos up and down both arms. He was wearing a dark green tee shirt and jeans and his expression, even when they were shaking hands, was distant. "This is Kevin Dunmore," said Duane. "And that's his significant other, Valerie."

Valerie was a redhead, shorter than Chloe, wearing a short tight skirt with a plaid pattern and a black halter top. She had piercings in her nose and lips and a tattoo wrapped itself around her neck. She regarded Chloe with obvious interest but nodded, saying nothing. Chloe felt a little bit out of place but there was a tub of beer buried in ice and she accepted one gratefully. It gave her something to do other than stand around trying to think of something to say.

The next two hours were more than slightly awkward. Duane managed the grill while the other three stood around and watched. No one said very much and no one seemed to find that at all strange.

Chloe felt as though she was in some kind of freefall. She didn't like not knowing what was going on. In fact, she didn't like not directing what was going on. She made a couple of tentative efforts to start a conversation but the others slipped away artlessly and returned to their silence. Even worse, she had the feeling that the other three were sharing some pertinent knowledge that was concealed from her, and that bothered her even more. She hated surprises unless she was arranging them, or at least privy to them in advance.

"You know, Duane, I'm starting to get a headache. I get migraines, you know. Would you mind if I cut out?"

His face was more animated than she had ever seen it. "I'm sorry. Can I get you some aspirin? You really should stay just a little bit longer. There's something I want to show you, something I arranged specially for today."

Chloe was torn. As awkward as she felt, she recognized that this might be her first real opportunity to learn something more personal about Duane. "Well, I can stay a little longer, I guess."

"Great!" He glanced at his wristwatch. "Everything should be ready in about half an hour."

Although Chloe was not nearly as sensitive to other people's moods as she believed herself to be, it would have been difficult not to notice the growing anticipation among her three companions. Obviously Kevin and Valerie were in on the secret. She was starting to feel the first glimmer of anger but she was determined not to show it, and not to react, particularly when it was revealed.

The time had come apparently because there was a sudden stirring. Duane took out his key chain and walked over to the shed. He undid the padlock. "Come on, Chloe. You really don't want to miss this."

Curious despite herself, she joined him, but not too eagerly. The other two trailed behind.

The doors swung wide and Chloe saw the origin of the strange noise she had heard during her earlier visit. It was the same sound now, but lower and faster, a kind of throbbing susurration. The center of attention looked like a gigantic milky globe except that it was more oval than round. It didn't quite fill the shed, but more importantly, it floated about six inches off the ground, with no visible means of support. Just beyond stood a narrow table with four very old looking books lying open.

"What is it?" she whispered the question.

"It's the anteroom of the gods," said Valerie.

"The Great Old Ones who ruled the world once before and who are destined to do so again," said Kevin. "They have been forsaken for countless ages, forced to remain alone and unworshipped on a distant plane. But their exile is almost over."

"It's the key to infinity," said Duane. None of them had really answered her question.

"But what is it exactly?"

"Come look at it," Duane beckoned her forward and she hesitantly moved to his side. "It's the most beautiful thing in the world. Think of it as a kind of gateway. The gods will be coming through soon and we need your help."

"What exactly do you want me to do, and what's going to happen if I do it?"

"We have summoned one of the gods to open the gateway. The Great One will be here soon. But in order to open the door, we need to provide a key."

"What kind of key?"

"Your kind, actually," said Valerie. "A young virgin must enter the gateway to complete the link."

Chloe took a step back, but Kevin was right behind her, barring the way. "What makes you think I'm a virgin?"

"Oh, please," said Valerie. "You might as well be carrying a sign around."

Ignoring Valerie, she turned to Duane. "What happens to me then?"

Duane sighed. "You will be immolated in the ecstasy of his passage. It's an unparalleled honor."

"I think I'll pass." She was going to push past Kevin then, but the cloudy surface of the sphere, which expanded and contracted slightly to coincide with the murmuring, suddenly cleared. And then something began to take form inside, something dark and very large and oddly shaped.

"Our lord and master has heeded our call," announced Duane, staring with such intensity that he leaned forward.

At first Chloe thought it looked like the head of a goat, but then she noticed that the goat head was protruding out of the forehead of something much larger and less easily described. And there were other things moving about as the mistiness receded. It actually hurt her eyes to look at some of them.

Kevin took her by the arm and Chloe reached into her pocket with the other hand, then withdrew it, spinning on one heel, and directed the pepper spray at Kevin's eyes. He cried out and recoiled, relinquishing his grip. Duane looked stupefied for a second, then reached for her, and Chloe acted instinctively, remembering her training. She turned her body again and let his own momentum help flip him up and over. He fell into the pulsing globe without so much as a cry of surprise.

Kevin was stumbling around with one hand covering his face. He swung the other arm but instead of striking Chloe, it caught Valerie in the face as she rushed forward to help. There wasn't much room to maneuver, but Chloe crouched beneath his flailing arm, moved around behind him, and planted a foot in the small of his back. He managed one cry of dismay as she pushed him into the sphere, which was now swirling angrily. The goat browed form seemed to be closer but less distinct, like a picture with low resolution.

"You bitch!" Valerie had found a shovel somewhere and was stalking toward her. Her nose was bleeding. "You've ruined everything, but the gods will have you yet." Chloe caught the haft of the shovel with both hands and the two women struggled furiously. Once their position was the way she wanted it, Chloe abruptly let go as Valerie tried to force her into the roiling mists. Instead she threw up her arms, desperately trying to regain her balance, and fell out of sight.

The churning grew more violent than ever, then receded and the original translucence was quickly restored. The god, if god it was, was not coming to visit today. "I guess Valerie wasn't a virgin," she said aloud.

She was about to close and lock the shed doors behind her when she stopped, thought a bit, then went back inside and gathered up the four ancient books. The sphere had returned to its somnolent breathing by then, with no visible features inside. She fastened the padlock and drove home.

Back in her home office, she carefully shelved the four fragile tomes below her row of scrapbooks. Then she took a blank one out of a box in the corner. Duane's story of abandoned gods languishing unhappily in exile had struck a chord with her. Now there was someone who needed help.

It would make a great project.

SHADOW OVER R'LYEH

It is not to vindicate myself that I write these words, nor to convince you of my sanity simply to secure my release from this asylum. The bizarre series of events which led to my incarceration admittedly has had a deep psychological impact and my thoughts remain in disarray. Nevertheless, the implications of my experience are of such dire proportions that I feel constrained to exert continuing efforts to convince someone, anyone, that my ravings have a foundation in fact, and that grave consequences are in store for us all unless steps are taken immediately to avert disaster.

It started many cycles ago, when I first left my small home den of Thuggeth to attend the University of R'lyeh in order to pursue my studies of the ancient sciences. I had received a small stipend as a consequence of my investigations into the cultural evolution of the Tcho and had received a personal letter of commendation from Administrator Nyarlathotep himself. He assured me that Supreme Chancellor Cthulhu himself was aware of my work and had written a note to the scholarship committee. I do not refer to these events to puff up my dorsal crest, but simply to demonstrate that my work has received serious recognition.

The university was a wonderful environment for me, and I threw myself into my studies with a vengeance. During my third cycle, I became interested in the archaeological aspects of Arcanology, having found clear evidence that much knowledge possessed by our ancestors was lost as a result of the cataclysmic events which resulted in our forced migration from the old universe. During several field trips, I became aware of the persistent belief, admittedly held among the lowest classes, that a bridge back to that vermin infested universe might still exist, access available only through the performance of certain questionable rituals. My initial revulsion at the prospect of contact with the usurpers of our rightful home diminished over a period of time, as I discovered bits and pieces of the knowledge that has been lost, tantalizing tidbits of no value in themselves.

During my fifth cycle at the university, I was summoned before the Chancellor Yog-Sothoth personally and told that there was danger of an imminent resumption of hostilities with the

Ancient Ones, those strange but normally remote entities who dominated this plane entirely prior to our arrival. I could tell by the nervous twitching of his tentacles that the Chancellor was under far more strain than he admitted, and a tremor of anxiety caused all three of my hearts to miss a beat. Desperate for some new weapon which might tip the balance in our favor, the government was providing financial support for a wide variety of projects, including my longstanding proposal to investigate rumors of supernaturally empowered artifacts in the Shunned Lands.

I made great haste to mount the expedition, fearing that a change in the political climate might cut off my funding at any moment. For that reason, I was somewhat less rigorous in my screening of those who would accompany me, a failing which had disastrous consequences, as you shall hear in due course. We made our way to the Shunned Lands without noteworthy incident, leaving the last outposts of civilization behind us and establishing a base camp just outside a forest of hideous evergreens. It was relatively far removed from the actual site we wished to examine, but the native bearers flatly refused to enter that coniferous jungle, even when we threatened to beat them. This meant that the four civilized members of our party were reduced to personally transporting our equipment to the actual excavation.

The very intensity with which the locals avoided this area was strong evidence that there existed here a nodal point linking the two universes. Our civilized senses may have been dulled, but these unspoiled primitives were still in touch with the primordial forces of creation. Among themselves, they freely discussed the legendary convulsion that cast us adrift in time and space, shut off from our home universe which was already being rapidly overrun by fast breaking, repulsive creatures with heated blood, too few limbs, and alien desires. Many of my colleagues had looked askance at my studies of ancient lore; an editorial in the departmental newsletter even characterized the expedition as a government sponsored "boondoggle". Nevertheless, I remained committed to my theory, and the skirmishing around Shuggat helped assure that my funding would not be withdrawn.

Nevertheless, we were all growing rapidly discouraged at the lack of progress after two full quarter cycles, and two of my assistants had actually requested permission to return to the university. It was with great relief and satisfaction then that I personally unearthed a viable artifact early one morning. Upon examination, it proved to be a volume of arcana, the notes of one of our ancestors who had made an effort to study the process by which we had been forced into exile. Although the scrolls were crumbling and incomplete, we were able to read several large fragments and found references to "Blokk" and "Klarkashton", two of the major supernatural entities referred to in the <u>Animacon,</u> a scroll reputedly so obscene and foul that even I have only been allowed to read certain excerpts.

To this day I regret the duplicity of my treacherous assistant Sarnath; he would not normally have been my choice for a companion on such a project and had I not been in such haste to depart, I would certainly have replaced him with someone of greater maturity. As it happened, only a favorable coincidence helped me avert a greater disaster than that which has already taken place.

We had just received word of the brilliant success of General Harlo-Optem in turning back a thrust from the border forces of the Ancient Ones and I was restless, concerned that my grant would be revoked under less threatening circumstances. All of my companions, I thought, were estivating but I was strangely animated, decided to take a short slither to soothe myself. On a whim, I turned my cilia toward the excavation site, although it was far too bright to accomplish anything there. I originally planned a short jaunt, but once within that crepuscular shroud of illuminated forest, I heard the distinct sound of music in the distance. Nor was it a healthy dirge or mantra but rather an unwholesome tonal melody which caused the slime to fall rom my back and sent a warm thrill up both of my spines.

I moved forward with caution, and it seemed an endless period before I reached the source of that unholy sound. I immediately recognized Sarnath, crouching at the bottom of one of the deeper of our digs. It was he who crooned this odious tune, occasionally breaking off to utter invocations to the forbidden entity, Luvkraft.

Suddenly I realized what he was attempting. Sarnath was a member of the outlawed cult of Arkhamists. That demented group believed that they were fated to open the doorway between universes so that the demonic vermin of that plane could enter our own, upsetting the existing order and rewarding the Arkhamists by making them our rulers.

I slithered forward, crying out in pure horror.

As it happened, I was just barely in time. Even as my mandibles closed around Sarnath's throats, my uppermost eyes observed a strange apparition forming in the haze. I cannot adequately describe the sense of alien menace I felt upon seeing that malformed monstrosity of only four limbs, totally devoid of tentacles or cilia, with but a single head, all enclosed in nauseating swatches of processed organic matter. Its unhealthy odor permeated the air and I retched uncontrollably. Convulsions wracked my body during one of which I fortunately severed all three of Sarnath's four heads.

As his concentration faltered, the manifestation dimmed; as fear retreated from my mind, I quickly finished off my erstwhile assistant. Although the link was terminated, my mind had undergone a great shock in the process, and I retreated temporarily into the safety of madness. When the rest of our party came looking for us the following morning, I was crawling through the forest, covered with hideous leafery from head to tentacles, my cilia matted with the Sarnath's ichor. With the evidence provided by his rapidly warming body and the absence of any concrete evidence of my motives, they naturally concluded that I had gone mad. The expedition was aborted and I was reduced to my present circumstances.

They treat me well here at the asylum, even allow access to the current news. I have heard of the renewed assault by the Ancient Ones. The recent setbacks along our border have apparently caused the government to approach the university about organizing a new expedition to complete my work.

It is with this last fact that I must deal now. They must dig no further into the past. The tenuous wall between the universes is already weakened at that spot; further meddling might well create a permanent rent in the fabric of reality. As unhappy as our fate might be should the Ancient Ones subjugate us, it is infinitely preferable to the result should those hideous denizens of the other universe be loosed upon us.

I pray that someone will heed my words and halt this insane project before it is too late.

www.ingramcontent.com/pod-product-compliance
Lightning Source LLC
Chambersburg PA
CBHW051240170626
46809CB00004B/1415